"This isn't a good idea."

"Hmm." Paige leaned into his hands, forcing him to support her full weight. Her fingers found another button and slipped it loose.

"I'm not a good man, Paige. I've done things you couldn't imagine."

"That's okay." Her palm stroked his chest, her fingers threading through the mat of hair. Jake swallowed hard, trying to remember what he was trying to say.

"I'm leaving in the fall."

"I know." His shirt hung open and her fingers were busy unbuckling his belt.

"This can't be anything more than a summer affair."

"I know." The rasp of his zipper sounded loud in the quiet room.

"I don't want to hurt you." The words were hardly more than a whisper.

She lifted her eyes to his face at last. The moonlight caught in her eyes, making them deep pools of mystery.

"I'm not asking you for anything more than tonight, Jake."

ABOUT THE AUTHOR

Dallas Schulze is a full-time writer who lives in Southern California with her husband and their two Persian cats. An avid reader, she devours books by the boxful. In what little spare time she has she enjoys doll collecting, old radio shows, classic and current movies, doll making, sewing, quilting and baking.

Books by Dallas Schulze
HARLEQUIN AMERICAN ROMANCE

DALLAS SCHULZE

A SUMMER TO COME HOME

Harlequin Books

TORONTO • NEW YORK • LONDON
AMSTERDAM • PARIS • SYDNEY • HAMBURG
STOCKHOLM • ATHENS • TOKYO • MILAN

Published November 1990

ISBN 0-373-16368-1

Chapter One

Jake Quincannon was back in town.

The news filtered through Riverbend with a speed military commanders would have envied.

Ethel Levine got the scoop on everyone else by virtue of the fact that Maisie's Café, where she worked, was located near the edge of town. Anyone entering or leaving Riverbend had to drive past Maisie's so Ethel was in a position to keep tabs on who was going where and with whom. Not that she was nosy. She would have been indignant if anyone ever suggested such a thing. She was just interested.

If it had been a busier time of day she might have missed seeing him, but at two o'clock on a Tuesday afternoon, Maisie's didn't do a booming business and she had time off from her job as Maisie's sole waitress to look out the big front window and watch the doings on Maine Avenue. Of course, as she explained to her five very closest friends at the Curl and Twirl Beauty Salon, the big Harley-Davidson was enough to catch a body's eye, even at a busy time of day. But this wasn't a busy time of day, so there was no need to worry about the possibility of missing anything.

Still, she might not have recognized the rider if it hadn't been for the light at the corner of Maine and Maple turning red at just the right moment. The big bike had coasted to a stop behind Fred Turley's Chevy pickup. It was rumored that Fred's four-year-old son had gotten his start in the back of that very pickup. Ethel studied the rusted bed for a moment before turning her attention to the new—and more interesting—vehicle behind it.

Like the motorcycle the rider was big and his hair was black. Thick and a little too long, in her opinion, it brushed the collar of his leather jacket. Worn jeans covered a pair of long legs, which were braced on either side of the bike. He wore black boots, as worn as the jeans.

Ethel sniffed, and pursed her thin lips disapprovingly. A thug. That's what he looked like. Just like the hired muscle the villains always had on television. Heaven knows what kind of big city filth he had hidden in the canvas duffel bag he'd strapped across the back of the bike. A gun, certainly. Maybe drugs.

Her speculations might have carried her even further if the man in question hadn't turned his head just then and looked directly at her.

Ethel gasped, too shocked to back away from the window. She gaped at the black leather patch that covered the man's left eye, giving him a villainous look. But it wasn't the patch or the thick black mustache that made her heart jump with shock.

Nearly twenty years had passed since she'd seen him but she recognized him immediately. There was something in the way he looked at her, one dark eyebrow cocked in arrogant amusement, that left her with no doubts about his identity. An unkind person might have suggested that Ethel's identification was aided by the fact that Margaret Quincannon had mentioned there was a possibility her eldest son might be coming home. But Ethel was sure she would have recognized Jake Quincannon even if they'd met in Timbuktu. There was just no mistaking the man. The way he lifted one black-gloved hand to his forehead in a mock salute confirmed his identity.

That arrogant gesture was pure Jake Quincannon, full of insolence and defiance. The boy had been trouble from the word go and Ethel now had proof that nothing had changed. She stepped back from the window but the move was wasted on the man riding the Harley. The light had changed to green and he lifted his booted foot from the pavement, giving the big bike gas as Fred Turley's truck started across the intersection.

Ethel craned her neck to get a final look at the bike as it disappeared down the road. Heading toward his folk's place, no doubt. Well, Lawrence and Margaret might or might not be glad to see the return of their prodigal son, but Ethel knew, as sure as if she were one of them psychics, that Jake Quincannon's return wasn't likely to be good news for anyone else.

Long before the dinner hour, most of Riverbend was aware of Jake's return. Those who'd lived in the town long enough to remember the elder Quincannon boy, shook their heads, wondering what mischief he might get up to this time. One or two kinder people ventured to point out that all that mischief was nigh on to twenty years ago now. Even Jake was bound to have settled down some by now. But there wasn't much support for this theory. Once a troublemaker, always a troublemaker.

Besides, who knew what he'd been up to all these years? It was a fact that the Quincannons were pretty closemouthed about Jake's doings. Government work, they said and that could cover most anything. It didn't seem likely that Jake had been toting up accounts for the past twenty years. More likely he'd been looking up trouble.

The news spread through town faster than a chicken could jump a june bug. It reached Paige Cudahy an hour or so before she was due to close the doors of Riverbend's tiny library. She was stacking books on the library's only book cart, preparatory to putting them back on the shelves.

Her movements were unhurried. Paige rarely felt that hurrying accomplished much. It was simply not a part of her makeup, a fact that had caused her endless conflicts with her older sister.

Josie believed that anything worth doing was worth doing quickly. Whether it was reading a book or bandaging a child's skinned knee, there was no sense in taking any more time than necessary. Time, to Josie's way of thinking, was a precious commodity to be used carefully.

Paige had simply never seen life quite the same way. She agreed that time was precious, but it was something to be savored, like a particularly rich piece of chocolate. It wasn't to be spent like coins, with a careful accounting made of each minute.

It wasn't the only thing the two sisters disagreed on, not by a long shot. In fact, it would have been hard to find something they *did* agree on.

Paige picked up a worn volume of Emerson's essays, and couldn't resist opening it, thumbing through to find a few favorite passages. The library was quiet.

The only patron was old Mr. Wellington and he was dozing in a corner near the window.

Standing between the stacks, surrounded by the faint musty scent of the books, Paige smiled. One of the things she liked best about running the library was the fact that there was no one telling her to pull her nose out of a book. All the years she was growing up, if it hadn't been her mother, it had been Josie, telling her that she was going to go cross-eyed from all that reading. Why couldn't she play with dolls, like other little girls?

"Paige Cudahy, get your nose out of that book. I've got the most fabulous news."

The piercing whisper made Paige jump and drop the book she was holding. It hit the wooden floor with a smack that echoed off the high ceilings, startling Mr. Wellington out of his nap. He snorted, his head jerking up, rheumy eyes peering out from under bushy white brows as he looked for the cause of the disturbance. Seeing nothing out of the ordinary, he settled back into the chair, his chin dipping toward his chest.

"Didn't anyone ever tell you that you shouldn't sneak up on a person?" Paige bent to pick up the book before turning to give Mary Davis a reproachful look.

"Wait till you hear what I've got to say." Mary grabbed Paige's arm, tugging her toward the front desk, her dark eyes flashing with excitement.

"If you're about to tell me that Mrs. Simms is a kleptomaniac, I've known that for years."

"Everybody knows that. Mr. Simms has been buying the stuff she's stolen for so long, it's a wonder the poor man hasn't gone broke."

"Maybe he's a drug dealer." Paige sat on the edge of her tiny desk, stretching her long legs out in front of her.

"Do you think so?" Mary was momentarily distracted from telling her news, intrigued with the idea that plump, balding Mr. Simms might be a drug kingpin. Paige watched her friend. She could practically see the wheels turning and she wondered if Mr. Simms was going to turn up as a character in one of Mary's books. She had been writing suspense novels for the past five years, and even though they'd all been rejected so far, she was determined to crack the doors of the publishing world wide open.

"I was only kidding about Simms," Paige said when the silence had dragged on long enough.

"But it could be true, don't you think?"

"Not unless he's selling crack to Holsteins. There aren't enough people around here to support Mrs. Simms's light fingers. The truth is that Mrs. Simms inherited quite a tidy sum from her grandfather. Some say that's why Mr. Simms married her. I suppose, if it's true, he got his comeuppance."

"Maybe he's planning to murder her for her money."

Paige raised her dark brows until they almost met the fall of her pale blond bangs. "After thirty years? He's waited a bit long, don't you think?"

"Maybe he hasn't gotten his courage up." Mary was reluctant to let go of a possible murder suspect.

"After this much time, I should think it wouldn't be worth the bother."

"I suppose." Mary was disappointed but she had to admit that Mrs. Simms's demise did not seem imminent.

Paige scooted farther onto the desk, crossing one knee over the other. "So, what's your news?"

"News?" Mary was still pondering the dramatic possibilities of the Simms household. "News!" She threw out her hands in a sharp gesture of exasperation. "How could I forget? Guess who just drove down Maine?"

"Tom Selleck."

"Don't be an idiot. This is someone you know. Actually, it's someone you used to know."

"Who said I couldn't 'used to know' Tom Selleck?" Paige asked lazily. The finish was wearing off the pine floor behind the desk. She was going to have to talk to the library committee about having the floor refinished.

"Well, it wasn't Tom Selleck. Guess again."

"Well..." Paige dragged the word out, giving it several syllables. "I suppose it's a safe bet it wasn't Robert Redford. And I know it couldn't have been Errol Flynn."

"He's been dead for thirty years."

"I know." Paige grimaced. "Think how unpleasant he'd look these days."

"Do you want to know who's back in town or don't you?" Mary scowled at her, but her eyes were laughing.

"I thought you wanted me to guess, and I'm doing my best." She ducked the small fist her friend raised. "Okay, okay. I give up. Who did you see driving down Maine?"

"Well, Ethel Levine saw him first and she told Gussie Marstan, who told Prissy Taylor, who told—"

"You can skip all that. I know the pattern the gossip mill runs in this town. Remember, I was born here.

Besides, after the news has passed through all those hands, it's hardly a reliable source. God knows, Yasser Arafat could become Wayne Newton by the time his name had passed down *that* route."

"Well, this happens to be true," Mary told her with a trace of huffiness.

"What happens to be true? So far, you haven't told me anything."

"Ethel was looking out the window of Maisie's and she saw this big black motorcycle and you'll never guess who was riding it."

Paige rolled her eyes in exaggerated impatience. There was nothing Mary loved more than dragging out the suspense. In fact, that was one of the problems with her books.

"Mary, you have precisely ten seconds to tell me who you're talking about and then I'm going to close up the library and lock you in here with Mr. Wellington. They say he was quite a ladies' man in his day."

Not visibly impressed by the threat, Mary cast a quick look at the somnolent old man.

"You're no fun, Paige."

"Mary—" Paige slid off the desk, her movement in Mary's direction underscoring her ominous tone.

"Jake Quincannon." Mary rushed the name out, stopping Paige's threatening approach instantly.

"Jake Quincannon? Are you sure?" Paige sank back onto the desk, her surprise all that Mary could have hoped for.

"Ethel saw him plain as daylight. He was riding a motorcycle and wearing a black leather jacket. And he had a patch over one eye." Mary clearly considered the last piece of information the cherry on the sundae.

"A patch? I wonder what happened?"

"I don't know. But Ethel said he looked meaner than a junkyard dog. Said he sent shivers right up her spine."

"Almost anything sends shivers up that woman's spine," Paige said with disgust. "Maybe she has a neurological problem."

Mary giggled. "I'd like to see you suggest that to her."

"Maybe one of these days I will." Paige leaned against the desk, her expression thoughtful. "Quincannon. Lord, it must be twenty years since he left Riverbend."

"Weren't he and Josie real tight?"

"They dated in high school. Everyone thought they were going to get married. Everyone thought it was a terrible idea. Josie was the prom queen and Jake— Well, Jake wasn't really the prom type. He rode a motorcycle then, too. His hair was too long, he was too tough. But Josie seemed crazy about him. I think my parents had just about resigned themselves to having Jake in the family."

She stopped, her gray eyes focused on things Mary couldn't see. Paige had been a child when Jake left town for the last time but he was vivid in her memory—a dark, brooding boy who'd always taken the time to talk to his girlfriend's bookish little sister.

"So what happened?" Mary prodded impatiently. "Why didn't Josie marry him?"

Paige shook the memories away and shrugged. "I don't know. Jake left to join the army. He was hardly out of sight before Josie was suddenly spending every waking moment with Frank Hudson. By the time Jake came home a couple of months later, Josie and Frank were married. There was a terrible fight. I was hiding in the hydrangea next to the porch and I could hear them arguing. Of course, there wasn't really much to say. After all, Josie and Frank *were* married. Then Jake took off and hasn't been back since."

"Wow. Didn't you ever ask Josie why she married Frank?"

Paige raised her brows. "*Me* ask Josie why she did something? I don't think so. Besides, I was only a kid when it happened. I didn't totally understand what happened until years later."

"I wonder why he's come back," Mary asked rhetorically, her ever-fertile imagination at work on half a dozen possibilities, each one more outlandish than the last.

"His parents are still here."

"I think this Jake Quincannon sounds like exactly what Riverbend needs to liven things up. It looks like it may turn out to be an interesting summer, after all."

Paige watched Mary leave, her small figure always in a rush, eager for the next experience life might offer her. She stared at the door long after it had closed behind her friend.

Jake Quincannon. A name out of the past. She wondered if Josie had heard the news yet. And how she'd react to it. Mary was right. It should be a very interesting summer, indeed.

JAKE COASTED THE BIKE to a stop at the end of the gravel driveway. Bracing the bike with one foot, he nudged the kickstand into place. Once the Harley rested securely, he reached up to lift off his helmet, running his fingers through his thick black hair.

The house sat on the edge of town, the valley sweeping away behind it, the mountains rising in the background. Snow capped the highest peaks, but summer had come to the lower levels.

The house hadn't changed, not in the twenty years he'd been gone, not in the twenty before that. The small lawn was a rich green, edged with neat flower borders. Fronting the modest house was a screened porch, and pots of calendula flanked the steps. Every year his mother would carefully place seeds in egg cartons and set the cartons next to the kitchen window. While the Idaho winter still howled outside, the tiny green seedlings held a promise of springtime.

Jake swung his leg over the bike, setting the helmet on the seat. His boot heels crunched on the gravel. Stepping onto the brick walk, he hesitated, wondering if coming back had been such a good idea.

Twenty years was a long time. Maybe he'd been a fool to think coming home could answer any of his questions. He reached up to touch the black leather patch that covered his left eye. Although the house hadn't changed in twenty years, a lot had changed in him.

With a mental shrug, he continued up the walk. He was here now, he couldn't really turn around and leave, though that was exactly what he felt like doing. Maybe it was mid-life crisis that had driven him to go back to his roots. His mouth twisted in a cynical smile. If he'd had any roots here, they'd died from lack of care a long time ago.

He knocked on the door, another thing that had changed. Twenty years ago, he'd have walked right in. But he didn't live here anymore. He was a visitor, probably an unwelcome one.

Footsteps came toward the door and Jake tensed, his stomach tightening the way it always did when he knew he was walking into a dangerous situation. He shoved his hands into his rear pockets and held his shoulders back as he waited for the door to open.

The man who opened the door was like a blurred photograph of the one he remembered. The years had not been kind to Lawrence Quincannon. Twenty years of riding ditch and peering into the rising sun, had etched themselves into his face. Deep lines fanned out from eyes that had faded to a lighter shade of blue than his son's. His hair, once as black as the obsidian that veined the hills behind him, was now completely gray.

The two men faced each other through the screen, each measuring two decades of change. Jake knew the years hadn't been much kinder to him than they had been to his father. Gray was sprinkled through the black of his hair; his face was hard. It took a conscious effort for him to control the impulse to reach up and check his eye patch.

"Jake."

"Dad." The word felt strange on his tongue.

"When you wrote, you didn't say just when you'd be getting here."

"I didn't know. I wanted to see a bit of the country on my way."

His father's eyes went over his shoulder to the big bike in the driveway and, for just a moment, his eyes lit with old memories. "Still riding one of those two-wheeled things, I see."

"No better way to see the country." Jake half smiled, remembering how his mother had protested the purchase of his first motorcycle. And how his father had supported him. They'd been almost close then.

"Lawrence, who is it?" The voice broke the tentative rapport with a force out of all proportion to its light, sweet sound. Jake tensed again, the knot in his stomach tightening.

"It's Jake, Mother." Silence greeted his words. With a half sigh, Lawrence opened the screen door. "Come on in, Jake."

Jake stepped through the door, his heavy boots loud on the polished hardwood floor. He drew in a deep breath, tasting the mingled scents of floor wax, baking and the lavender potpourri his mother had always loved. It was a combination that swept him back to his childhood. He was five and he'd just lost a frog in the hallway. He was twelve and his mother was furious at the mud he'd tracked over her newly polished floors. He was eighteen and leaving for the army and she was watching him with those guarded eyes that never quite seemed to see him.

"Mother is in the parlor." His father's voice dragged him away from his memories and Jake nodded, following the slightly stooped figure down the short hallway. He stopped in the doorway, aware that he didn't feel any differently now than he had when he was sixteen and about to be called on the carpet for some perceived crime.

Margaret Quincannon was sitting in her favorite chair, the one that caught the pure northern light. Her hair had gone from pale blond to light gray but it was still pulled back in the same soft bun she'd always worn. Her pink floral housedress was identical to the ones she'd worn during his childhood. The pile of knitting in her lap could have been the same yarn she'd held twenty years ago.

Her face was older, more lined, but her eyes were the same watchful gray he remembered. She looked at him as if wondering what he was going to do next. It was that look that had so often driven him to his most outrageous pranks, as if by fulfilling her expectations, he could somehow make her love him.

"Jacob." Her voice held neither welcome nor rejection. She was simply acknowledging his presence, nothing more.

"Hello, Mother." Before he could stop the gesture, he reached up to adjust the patch. He lowered his hand, cursing the vulnerability she could still make him feel.

"Come in and sit down." That was his father, settling into the chair across from his wife's, reaching for his pipe.

Jake crossed the worn carpet and sat on the sofa. It was the same hideously uncomfortable affair he remembered from childhood. And it was also his mother's pride and joy. He was aware of her watching him carefully as he tried to adjust his long frame to the rigid back and narrow seat.

"It's been a long time," Lawrence said, breaking the silence before it could grow to uncomfortable proportions. "We got your postcards. Seems like you did a good bit of traveling."

"Quite a bit." Jake gave up trying to be comfortable and settled for the least uncomfortable position he could find.

"Sounds nice." Lawrence tamped tobacco into his pipe.

"I enjoyed it."

"What happened to your eye?" Margaret asked over the click of her knitting needles, her eyes on her work.

"I lost it." Jake jerked his hand down halfway to the patch, feeling the familiar helpless rage his mother had always brought out in him.

"In a fight, I suppose." Her light, sweet voice was laced with contempt. Lawrence continued to focus on tamping down the tobacco in his pipe.

"As a matter of fact, it was a fight," Jake said, a challenging edge to his voice. "I suppose I should consider myself lucky, though. He was trying for my neck. Of course, there are those who might consider it a shame he missed."

"No one said anything about wishing you dead, Jacob." Margaret's needles continued to click along rhythmically, never dropping a stitch.

"No. But no one said anything about being glad I'm alive, either."

"Naturally, your father and I are glad you're alive. You're our son."

Lawrence cleared his throat before Jake could respond. "How long do you think you'll be staying in Riverbend, Jake?" His eyes pleaded with his son. Jake swallowed the lump of anger that threatened to choke him.

"I'm not really sure. Possibly for the summer. Maybe not as long as that."

"I can't imagine what a man like you would find to do in Riverbend for the summer," Margaret commented.

"But then you don't really know what kind of man I am, do you, Mother?"

"Where are you planning on staying?" Lawrence asked, verbally stepping between his wife and son. "You could have your old room, if you'd like."

Margaret's knitting needles hesitated, her fingers tightening on the thin wands. For one moment, Jake was tempted to say he'd stay in his old room, just because he knew nothing would please his mother less. But he hadn't come back to renew old feuds or open old wounds.

"Thanks, but I think it would be best if I found a place in town."

"There aren't many places to stay in Riverbend," Margaret commented.

"I'm sure I'll find something." He stood up. He felt stifled in this room. "Well, I guess I'll be going."

"You'll have to come to dinner, Jake." Lawrence stood up, his eyes showing a touch of anxiety.

"I'd like that, Dad. I'll let you know where I'm staying."

"Welcome home, son." Lawrence held out his hand. Jake took it, feeling the softness of old age in a grip that had once been rock hard.

"Thanks. Goodbye, Mother." Margaret looked up at her son, her expression remote.

"Goodbye, Jacob."

Jake stepped off the porch, drawing in a deep breath of warm air. He reached for the gloves he'd tucked into his back pocket. This had been a stupid idea. What had made him think he was going to find what he was looking for in Riverbend? Especially when he didn't even know what it was he was looking for. He tugged his helmet on, swinging his leg over the wide seat. The Harley started with a roar, as out of place in this sleepy little town as he was.

If he had any sense, he'd just take the road right back out of town and mark this little visit up to stupidity. He'd been called a lot of things in his time but sensible wasn't one of them. Stubborn was. He'd come home for the summer and he decided he wasn't going to leave before he'd even spent a single night here.

Chapter Two

Like everything else in Riverbend, the old Cudahy house hadn't changed much. It looked as if it needed more repairs than most of the houses, as if it had been a while since anyone had seen to the upkeep.

Old Mr. Cudahy had taken great pride in the smooth expanse of lawn that stretched from the porch to the sidewalk, in the immaculately clipped hedges that bordered the porch. The lawn was still green, but mowing was obviously not high on the current occupant's list of priorities. The hedges were gone and in their place were flowers, not neat little beds but wild tangles of blooms and color. Hollyhocks reached nearly to the porch roof, a stately background to the miniature jungle at their feet. The roses that had once marched in neat precision along the south side of the house now sprawled in extravagant abandon, their canes heavy with flowers, the scent almost overpowering in the warm air.

Jake leaned against the porch railing. There were memories here, too. How many times had he waited on this porch for Josie to come out, aware of her mother peering through the lace curtains at him, feeling her disapproval.

He half smiled. The clerk at the little store on the edge of town had said that Paige Cudahy owned the house now and that she sometimes rented rooms. The clerk had stared at him as if he were an alien, but she'd been forthcoming enough about the slightly scruffy index card he'd pulled off the bulletin board near the door.

Yes, the room was available, she'd told him, her fascinated gaze drawn to the patch over his eye. The last time Paige had had a boarder was nearly a year ago. A writer had been looking for a quiet place to stay while he finished a book. Hadn't stayed long. Apparently Riverbend was quieter than he'd anticipated.

Jake had nodded his thanks, resisting the urge to shout ''boo'' just to see her scuttle for cover. Taking the card with him, he'd gone back out to the Harley, aware of her peering cautiously out the door after him.

Nothing ever changed in this town, it seemed. Gossip was still the major form of entertainment. When he was growing up here, it had been the bane of his life that you couldn't spit on the sidewalk without half the town knowing about it before the day was over.

He ran his fingers over the peeling paint on one of the pillars that supported the porch roof. He wondered how long Bill Cudahy had been dead. And Mrs. Cudahy? Was she still alive? The clerk had mentioned only Paige. That would be Josie's little sister.

He narrowed his eyes, staring absently at a fat bee making one last visit to an overblown rose before heading back to the hive. He vaguely remembered Paige. She'd been just a child when he left—maybe five or six, he thought. A plump little thing with long blond pigtails.

He couldn't remember Josie having much time for her, but then, time and distance had made him realize that Josie's attentions had usually been devoted to herself. Paige hadn't been of much use to her, so Josie had ignored her.

Paige would be—what? Twenty-four, twenty-five now. Idly, he wondered what she looked like. Was she still short and plump?

His gaze lit on a figure walking down the street. Pure male appreciation straightened his spine. This was a woman who'd turn heads anywhere she went. In Riverbend, she was enough to stop traffic. She was tall, about five eight, he judged. She was slim but with curves in all the right places. And her legs—her legs went on forever. The snug denim skirt she wore ended several inches above her knee, a length of which any man would heartily approve. She walked with a long lazy stride that made a man think of hot summer nights and cool sheets.

She reached up to flick a length of pale blond hair over her shoulder. When she turned her head to wave at a woman across the street, he could see that her hair fell thick and straight down her back, ending just above her waist. Straight bangs fringed over her forehead, almost touching her dark brows.

So absorbed was he in watching her that she'd taken several steps up the brick walkway before he realized that she was walking toward the house where he waited. He straightened away from the porch, disbelief edging out lust when he realized that *this* must be short, plump little Paige.

"Jake Quincannon." Her voice was low and husky, wrapping around his name in a way that evoked images of bedroom whispers. Her eyes were wide set and dark, pure green.

"Paige Cudahy?" The name was a question, though he didn't doubt her identity.

"The one and only," she said, moving past him up the steps and onto the porch. She glanced over her shoulder as Jake followed her.

"You've changed." It was the only comment that came to mind. It sparked a husky laugh as appealing as her voice. She turned, her hair swinging with the movement. Her eyes flicked over him.

"You've done a bit of changing yourself."

"You mean this?" Jake's hand moved before he could stop it, touching the black patch that covered his eye.

Her eyes swept up and down again. Her mouth quirked as her gaze met his. "That, but I was thinking more of the way you're dressed."

"The way I'm dressed?" Jake glanced down at himself.

"Really, Jake, you never used to be so obvious."

"Obvious?" He ground his teeth. He realized he was repeating everything she said, like a parrot. He'd had conversations with deposed kings and reigning terrorists and he'd always managed to sound reasonably intelligent. In the space of two minutes, Paige Cudahy—little Paige, for God's sake—had managed to throw him off balance.

"The clothes, Jake. Where did you get them? Central Casting for the returning rebel?" She flicked her fingers in his direction. "Boots, jeans, black T-shirt, even a leather jacket. It's good, I'll give you that." She tilted her head to one side, studying him with wide green eyes. "It suits you but it would have created more of an effect to try a three-piece suit. Ethel Levine might not even have recognized you. Or you could have tried linen slacks and one of those shirts with the little animals on them. In pink, maybe."

"Pink?" he asked, wondering if he'd missed a piece of this conversation somewhere.

"Okay, maybe not pink," she said easily.

She was teasing him. The idea was nearly as shocking as if she'd drawn a gun on him. A gun he'd have known how to handle. This light teasing tone wasn't so simple. He couldn't remember the last time someone had teased him.

"The problem is that you've done exactly what they expected you to do," she told him. "You should surprise people once in a while. It's good for them."

"Do you surprise people often?"

"Not too often. It takes too much energy. I believe in conserving energy, my personal contribution to the environment. I suppose you want to rent the room."

The abrupt change of subject seemed hardly worth noting. Jake nodded.

"You had a card on a bulletin board."

"Must have been yellow with age. Nobody's rented the place in nearly a year."

"So the girl at the counter told me."

"She probably told you that the last boarder was a writer. Said he wanted peace and quiet to finish his magnum opus. He sat up there two hours a day, pondering the fickleness of his muse and then he spent the other twenty-two hours drinking down at the Dew Drop Inn. He finally announced that the bucolic atmosphere was detrimental to his creative spirit and left. Is that your bike?"

"Yes." Jake was becoming accustomed to her erratic conversational style.

"It looks wonderful. I thought of getting one when I turned eighteen but my mother was convinced I'd end up with my lipstick smeared all over the highway and I gave up on the idea. Personally, I think it was your fault."

"Mine?"

"She never approved of you, you know. She thought you were going to encourage Josie to do things unbecoming to a prom queen. Actually, I think it would have done Josie a lot of good if someone had tarnished her crown a bit."

"What does that have to do with your mother not wanting you to get a bike?" She'd lost him again, just when he was sure he was following the conversation.

"A motorcycle reminded Mother of you, of course. Why don't you come in and you can take a look at the room."

She pushed open the door and Jake realized that it hadn't been locked, another thing that hadn't changed in the years he'd been gone. Half the people in town probably didn't even know where the key to their front door was.

Paige kicked off her shoes as soon as she stepped into the entryway. The house was warm after having been shut up all day and she made a mental note to leave a few windows open tomorrow. The oak floor was cool on her feet and she curled her toes against it. It was too bad she had to wear shoes to work. The weather simply cried out for bare feet.

But the library committee of Riverbend would never approve of the librarian going barefoot. They didn't entirely approve of her as it was, but the one time Mrs.

Hallard had ventured to suggest that her clothing wasn't really restrained enough for a librarian, Paige had threatened to quit. Since they were lucky to get someone with even part of an English degree, Mrs. Hallard had beat a hasty retreat.

Paige turned as Jake stepped in, shutting the screen behind him but leaving the door open. Funny, how the entryway seemed suddenly smaller. It wasn't just his size. Her father had nearly matched Jake Quincannon's six feet three inches and his presence had never made a room shrink.

No, there was something about Jake—an aura, Mary would probably say. The man simply commanded attention. It wasn't just the black leather jacket or the ominous patch over his eye. It was something that emanated from him, probably without his even being aware of it.

"Is something wrong?"

The question made her realize that she'd been staring. She smiled and shrugged, unconcerned about having been caught.

"I was just thinking that the room seems smaller with you in it. I can't wait for Mary to meet you. She's going to say that you have a special aura. She'll probably put you in one of her books. The room is upstairs."

"Mary?" Jake questioned warily.

"A friend of mine," Paige explained as she led the way upstairs. "She's going to sell a book one of these days. Just as soon as she learns that anticipation may make the heart grow fonder but it exhausts a reader. She writes suspense stories. She's been rejected by some of the very best publishers."

"Is that good?"

"Well, I guess it's better than being rejected by the worst."

"Is this part of the theory that if you're going to get hit by a car, it doesn't hurt as much if it's a Rolls?"

Paige turned as they reached the landing. "Why, Jake, I do believe that was a joke. And you're almost smiling. I have a feeling you don't do nearly enough of that. You should try it more often. It's very good for you."

She also had a feeling that it had been a long time since anyone had teased Jake Quincannon. Which was a pity. Everyone needed someone to keep them from taking themselves and the world too seriously.

She pushed open the door to what she grandly referred to as her rental unit. "This used to be Josie's room. When she moved out, my parents kept it more or less as a shrine but I'm not as sentimental as they were."

"It can't bring in much money, if you only rent it once a year."

"No, hardly enough to be worth the bother, I suppose. I just like to break up the monotony. Besides, my occasional tenants give the town something to talk about."

"They always used to find enough to talk about without anyone having to work at it," he commented, glancing around the large, plainly furnished room.

"But that was when you were in town. Once you left, they lost one of their favorite topics."

"Didn't someone come along to take my place?"

"Not really." She ran a finger over the top of the bureau, studying the pattern it created in the dust. "I suppose I should dust but it just gets dusty again.

You'd be responsible for your own room. I don't do sheets, or clothes, or windows. There's a dust mop in the hall closet and you're welcome to use the washer and dryer in the basement.'' She named a sum that seemed reasonable, less than he'd have paid to stay at the scruffy motel that was Riverbend's only facility for visitors.

"That sounds fair. Do you want a month in advance?"

"Whenever you get around to it. I'm in no hurry." She looked around, wondering vaguely if there wasn't something else she should tell him.

"Where does that door lead to?"

"The bathroom. We share it. I promise not to leave my underwear drying on the towel rack, if you'll promise not to leave shaving cream in the sink."

"I think I can manage that."

"Then we should get along just fine."

"Are those your only prerequisites for getting along with someone?"

"The most important ones. Why don't you bring up your stuff. I'll treat for dinner tonight."

Jake watched her leave the room, his eyes lingering on those incredible legs. Who would have thought that chubby little Paige would grow up into such a long-legged beauty?

Paige wandered back downstairs, went into the big kitchen at the back of the house and pulled a bottle of soda out of the ancient refrigerator. She heard Jake go through the front door as she was twisting off the cap. He came back in while she was rummaging through the freezer for something to cook. And then she could hear his footsteps overhead. She pulled out a frozen pizza and set it on the counter.

Funny, how she hadn't felt any real surprise when she'd seen him leaning against the porch. Unless he stayed at his parents' house, which hadn't seemed likely, this was about the only place in Riverbend to rent a decent room. But it wasn't logic that had made his presence seem natural.

How many times had she seen Jake standing in just that same place, waiting for Josie? He wasn't the tough boy he'd been twenty years ago and she wasn't the plump little girl who'd had such a terrible crush on her sister's boyfriend.

One thing that hadn't changed was the way her heart had given a funny little bump when she'd first seen him. For just a moment, she'd felt as breathless as she had twenty years ago. It had seemed almost inevitable to walk down the street and find him standing in front of the porch, waiting for her. As if all those vague childhood fantasies had finally come true.

The gossip mill must have gotten to Josie by now. In fact, she was probably one of the first people to hear about Jake's return. Twenty years may have passed but Riverbend hadn't forgotten that Josie and Jake had once been an "item."

As Jake came down the stairs, the smell of oregano and cheese wafted upward, announcing dinner. Pizza. He couldn't remember the last time he'd had pizza. Paige was setting out plates when he entered the kitchen. The radio was on, and he could make out Sam Cook through the scratchy reception.

Paige was humming along, singing a word here and there, her bare feet moving in rhythm to the mellow tune. There was a huge bouquet of flowers in the center of the big oak table. She hadn't bothered to arrange them in any particular order. It looked as if she'd simply wandered through the garden, picking whatever caught her eye, and stuffed them into a vase.

There were thick cloth napkins in a somewhat eye-searing pattern of purple and yellow and plates that didn't match. She hadn't bothered with any silverware, assuming that, like any civilized American, he understood that pizza was finger food.

She turned and saw him, ostensibly not in the least disturbed at being seen dancing while she was setting the table. She smiled, the expression starting in her eyes before moving to her mouth. It struck Jake that it had been a long time since he'd seen someone smile with their eyes.

"Decided to give up the retro-rebel look, huh?"

"For now. It isn't pink and there's no little animals on the pocket but it was the best I could do in a pinch."

She looked him up and down, taking in the jeans and the blue cotton shirt with the sleeves rolled halfway up his forearms. Sneakers had replaced the black leather boots. He'd combed his wavy hair into place but one rebellious wave had fallen onto his forehead.

"Nice," she announced, having given it serious consideration.

"Thanks," he said dryly. "I think the last woman to critique my wardrobe was my mother."

If Paige caught any sarcasm in his tone, she chose to ignore it. "The glasses are in the cupboard to the left of the fridge. I've got wine—aged at least a week in aluminum barrels. There's water, milk or soda."

"I think I'll stick with water, it sounds the safest of the bunch."

"Pour me a glass of milk, would you?" She was leaning over the oven as she spoke and Jake couldn't resist a lingering look at the rather extraordinary length of leg her skirt exposed.

He dragged his gaze away as she lifted the pizza out and straightened. Getting the glasses, that was what he was supposed to be doing. It wasn't until he was setting them on the table that he realized they were decorated with cartoon characters.

Paige scooped an enormous slice of pizza onto each plate and settled in the chair across from his. She lifted her wedge of pizza and took a bite. It wasn't until she had swallowed that she noticed Jake hadn't moved.

"Don't you like pizza?" She raised her brows, as if the thought was inconceivable.

"My glass has a picture of Tweety Bird."

"Don't you like him? I've got Sylvester and I don't think I've broken the Bugs Bunny yet."

He met her eyes and wondered if he looked as if he'd fallen into the Twilight Zone. What would the people he'd worked with over the past fifteen years think if they could see Jake Quincannon now? Sitting in a homey kitchen with a slice of pizza in front of him and drinking from a glass with a picture of Tweety Bird on it.

"He's fine," he said somewhat weakly. He reached for the pizza, unable to shake the feeling that there was something wrong with this picture.

Paige didn't seem to feel the need to make conversation to fill up the silence, a trait Jake admired. He'd never understood why people seemed to think that silence was dangerous. In his experience, it could be an ally.

Glancing across the table at Paige, he was struck by the fact that she seemed completely relaxed. People didn't usually feel so comfortable in his presence. His own parents had watched him as if he were a dangerous animal who might turn on them. For some reason, her calm acceptance of his presence was disturbing.

"Are you always this comfortable with strangers?" he asked abruptly.

"You're not really a stranger."

"You haven't seen me in twenty years. For all you know, I could have become an ax murderer." Jake couldn't explain his irritation.

"Have you become an ax murderer?" She didn't seem concerned with his answer and Jake scowled as he reached for another slice of pizza.

"You're too trusting."

"You take yourself too seriously." There was no bite in the words but they stung nevertheless.

"You don't know anything about me," he snapped.

"If you *were* an ax murderer, you'd hardly come back here to commit your dastardly deeds. The whole town is just waiting for you to sneeze crossways to prove that you turned into the criminal they all predicted you'd become. If you murdered me in my sleep, they'd hang you from the nearest tree without benefit of trial."

Jake set the glass down with a thump. "Doesn't it worry you?"

Paige eyed him over a slice of pizza that dripped cheese, her eyes a cool green. "Do you want me to be afraid of you, Jake? Would it feed your ego?"

"My ego? What does my ego have to do with it?"

"I get the feeling that you're used to people being afraid of you. If you've come home to prove that you've turned out just as wicked as they all predicted you would, don't start with me."

She stood up, took her plate over to the sink and rinsed it before setting it on the counter. Jake was still sitting at the table when she left the room, staring at the cold pizza, aware that he'd just made a total fool of himself. Maybe it had been too long since he'd had any dealings with real people. Maybe he didn't know how to behave like a normal person anymore.

He'd come home to find out who he was. Instead, he was finding out that he had the manners of a warthog. With a sigh, he shoved his chair back. Reaching for his glass, he had a fleeting wish that it held something more potent than water. When he set the glass down, Tweety seemed to be staring at him, his beak pursed in disapproval.

"Okay, so I blew it," Jake muttered. "Maybe they were right. Maybe you can't ever go back. She's probably going to throw me out on my ear and I can't say I would blame her."

He stared at the painted yellow bird, so absorbed in thought that it didn't even strike him that he was talking to a cartoon character. Reaching up to rub the back of his neck, he was conscious of a deep weariness that had little to do with the miles he'd travelled in the last few days.

He wasn't sure what he'd been expecting when he came home but Paige Cudahy hadn't been part of the picture. And neither had his reaction to her.

The only thing he was really sure of was that he didn't want her to ask him to leave.

Chapter Three

The house was quiet when Jake came downstairs the next morning. He assumed Paige had already gone to work, though he hadn't thought to ask where she worked. There were probably a lot of things he should have asked, instead of haranguing her for trusting a virtual stranger and renting him a room.

He hadn't seen her again last night after she'd left the kitchen. When he went upstairs, the door to her room had been shut and it hadn't seemed like a good idea to disturb her. Apologies were better made in the calm light of morning.

He strode into the kitchen, wanting nothing more than a cup of strong coffee. But the kitchen was occupied. Paige leaned on the counter as she watched a particularly fat sparrow gorging himself at the bird feeder that hung outside the window.

She hadn't heard him approach and Jake was glad of it. It probably wouldn't be the smartest move to start off his apology by staring at the stunning length of leg bared by a pair of very short shorts. Starting at her bare feet and traveling up over lightly tanned calves and thighs, his gaze lingered on the way the denim shorts molded the curves of her buttocks. The shorts were topped by a loose T-shirt in a shade of green that made him think of maple leaves in the spring.

It wasn't possible that Josie's little sister had grown up into this desirable woman. It wasn't fair. He shifted his weight and the oak floor creaked, announcing his presence.

"Good morning, Jake." Paige turned slowly.

"Good morning." Her expression was impossible to read. It occurred to him that, for all her seeming openness, there was a great deal of Paige Cudahy that was kept hidden.

"If you're hungry, there's Fruit Loops and Cocoa Puffs in the cupboard." She dipped her hand into the box of Cap'n Crunch she held, pulling out a handful. Jake controlled a shudder.

"Actually, all I really want is a cup of coffee."

"All I've got is instant." She pointed to the cupboard behind him. "It's pretty old. I only keep it for guests. All that caffeine is bad for you."

Jake glanced pointedly at the sugar-coated cereal she was munching.

"Sugar is an energy food," she said defensively, looking as if energy was the last thing she had any interest in acquiring.

"Caffeine is a sanity food," Jake said, finding a pan in the cupboard she pointed to with one bare foot. He filled the pan with water and set it on the stove, turning the flame as high as possible. He was aware of Paige watching him as he dumped coffee into a thick mug.

Neither of them spoke until Jake had poured the hot water over the coffee crystals and had taken his first swallow of the nearly scalding liquid.

Feeling as if he just might live another day, Jake eyed Paige over the rim of the mug. She looked completely relaxed, her hips braced against the counter, her long legs crossed at the ankles. She'd pulled her hair back into a thick braid that fell over one shoulder, leaving only the slightly ragged bangs to frame her eyes. At first glance she looked about fourteen—but only at first glance. There was nothing girlish about the warm curves of her figure, nothing childlike in the sensuous shape of her mouth.

Jake took another swallow of coffee, grimacing at the stale taste. She hadn't been kidding when she said it was old. He cradled the warm mug between his palms.

"Look, I'm sorry about last night." At his abrupt apology, Paige glanced up from the box of cereal. "I guess I haven't spent enough time in polite company these last few years." He shrugged, his mouth twisting. "And maybe you're right, maybe I am used to people being afraid of me. Anyway, I had no business jumping down your throat."

"No, you didn't." But there was no anger in the words. "Why *did* you come home, Jake?"

He couldn't even answer that question for himself. "I don't know exactly. Maybe I just wanted to see if it had changed."

"Riverbend never changes. It won't take you very long to find that out."

"Well, I've got the summer. I decided to take the summer to come home and find..." He shrugged, not knowing exactly what he hoped to find. "...whatever."

"I hope you find your whatever, Jake. I don't think most people even know when they've lost it." She smiled as she made her statement, and Jake wondered if it was his imagination that saw a fleeting look of discontent in her eyes.

The screen door pushed open before he could pursue the thought any further. The girl who breezed in was in her late teens and pretty enough to turn heads. Her dark hair was cut short, framing a pair of deep blue, thickly lashed eyes.

"Hi, Aunt Paige." Though she spoke to Paige, her eyes were on Jake. "You must be Jake Quincannon. I'm Beth. Everybody says you and Mom used to be a hot item. She never told me you were so good-looking."

"Beth, you have the manners of a chimpanzee," Paige told her dryly, rescuing Jake from the necessity of finding a reply. "Jake, this is Josie and Frank's daughter, as you've probably already guessed. Someone once told her that honesty was the best policy and so she abandoned all efforts at developing any tact or discretion."

"You're the one who said that people should always express their thoughts, Aunt Paige." Beth threw her aunt a mischievous look. Paige responded by throwing a towel at her. Beth caught the towel, grinning at her before turning to Jake.

"Should I apologize for having said that you're good-looking?" The offer was made so demurely that Jake found himself unable to resist her youthful charm.

"I think I can bear up under the burden," he said, giving her a half smile.

"Don't encourage her, Jake," Paige told him lazily. "She's the bane of the family as it is." She caught the wadded towel Beth tossed back at her. "What are you doing here, anyway? I thought you were going to work at the bank this summer.''

"I am, but I don't start till next week. Billy and I are going on a picnic and I asked him to pick me up here.''

The last part of the sentence came out in a rush. Annoyance flickered in Paige's eyes.

"I thought your parents didn't want you seeing him.''

"Mom and Dad are such sticks-in-the-mud. You know they are, Aunt Paige.''

"Whether that's true or not, I don't want you using this house to meet Billy behind their backs.''

This was a new side to Paige—the stern aunt. Jake took a sip of coffee, watching the little drama unfold. Beth shifted uneasily beneath Paige's severe look.

"They can't make me stop seeing Billy. And neither can you.''

"I'm not going to try and make you do anything. But I don't want you meeting him here again.''

Beth hesitated, her face flushed with anger and embarrassment. But there was no arguing with that look and she knew it.

"All right.''

A hiccuping roar in the street outside shattered the slightly tense silence. Beth brightened immediately, her eyes sparkling.

"There's Billy now. I won't do it again, Aunt Paige. It was great to meet you, Jake.'' A flash of tanned legs and she was gone.

Paige sighed, moving over to the counter to heap instant coffee into a cup. She reached for the water Jake had left on the stove.

"I thought you didn't drink coffee,'' he commented.

"I said it wasn't good for you. I didn't say I didn't drink it." She poured water over the coffee and took a swallow, grimacing at the taste.

"Pretty girl," Jake said, not sure why he was lingering. Hadn't he decided last night that it might be a good idea to keep some distance between himself and his landlady?

"She's usually intelligent, too. But this Billy—" Paige broke off, shaking her head. "For once, I agree with Josie. He's no good for Beth."

"Sounds familiar. Everyone said the same thing about me and Josie." His smile was rueful. "And they were probably right."

"No one ever said you were a creep," Paige said firmly. "They might have said you were wild and destined to come to a bad end, but no one ever said you were a creep. Billy Wilson is a creep."

It was clear that to her the former was preferable to the latter. Jake didn't question her logic.

"She'll probably figure that out herself, sooner or later," he said easily, glad it wasn't his problem.

"I hope so." Paige fixed him with a speculative look, the coffee in her hand forgotten.

"Did you come back here because of Josie?"

"Josie?" The question surprised him. "Why would I come back because of Josie?"

"Well, you were madly in love with her."

"It was a long time ago. I was nineteen."

"You were furious when you came back to find she'd married Frank. I was hiding behind the hydrangea listening."

Jake frowned, trying to remember how he'd felt. "I think I was more hurt that Frank would marry my girl than that Josie married Frank. He was my best friend.

When you're a nineteen-year-old boy, best friends aren't supposed to do that kind of thing." He shrugged and finished the last of his coffee. "As I've already said, it was a long time ago. Whatever I felt then is long gone, including any puppy love I had for your sister."

HIS MIND was still on the conversation half an hour later as he pushed open the door of Riverbend's only bank. He seemed to be thinking about Paige Cudahy more than he had any business doing. Shaking his head, he reached for the envelope that stuck carelessly out of the back pocket of his black jeans.

"Jake Quincannon." Startled, Jake stiffened at the gruff sound of his name, his hand twitching instinctively toward the gun he no longer wore. He turned slowly, his wary expression easing into a smile that would have surprised many who were convinced they knew him.

"Pop! You old dog, I thought they'd have put you out to pasture years ago."

He reached out to grip the other man's hand. Pop Bellows had been one of the few people Jake could have called a friend twenty years ago. He'd seemed positively ancient then, though he probably hadn't been much over fifty.

"Hell, they made me retire but they couldn't make me sit at home waiting to die." Pop's eyes had faded and his skin had the worn look of old leather but the hand Jake gripped was still firm and strong. "I took over as security guard here when old Smitty had a heart attack."

All Jake had seen at first was that Pop was still wearing a uniform, just as he had twenty years ago.

Now he noticed that the uniform wasn't the tan he'd worn as the town's sheriff. This was a crisp navy blue.

"Who's keeping law and order now that you've retired?"

"You remember Martin Smith? Well, he joined the Marines a year or two after you left. When he got out, he came back home and settled down. Turned into a pretty fine officer. Trained him myself."

"You probably scared him into doing a good job," Jake said. "Just like you scared me into staying out of trouble."

"Some folks learn without having to have the fear of God put into them." Pop gave him a pointed look. "Don't look like you remembered everything I taught you. What happened to your eye?"

Jake reached up to touch the leather patch. He didn't mind the question coming from Pop, knowing that there was more than idle curiosity behind it. "I zigged when I should have zagged."

"Well, I'd guess it doesn't do you any harm with the ladies," the old man said. "They're bound to think it makes you look like a pirate or some such nonsense. What are you doing home after all these years? What's it been? Fifteen, sixteen years?"

"Almost twenty, Pop."

"That long?" Pop shook his head. "The older I get the faster time goes. So what are you doing home, Jake?"

"I don't know. It seems like everybody's asked me that and I still don't know the answer. It seemed like as good a place as any to spend the summer, I guess."

"Well, I suppose Riverbend ain't a bad spot to light for a while. I'm not sure I ever expected to see you back here though. I figured once you shook the dust of this town off your feet, you weren't likely to come back.''

"Maybe I came back for some more of that lethal lemon cake of yours."

Pop looked blank for a moment, then his eyes widened and he laughed. "I'd nearly forgotten that cake."

"I'm not likely to forget. Not when it damn near killed me. I hope you've been staying away from the kitchen. Otherwise, the cemetery must be just about full of your victims."

"Now, Jake, I was trying to do you a favor," Pop protested, still chuckling.

Jake's smile softened. Funny how he'd almost forgotten the reason Pop had baked that inedible cake. It had been to celebrate his graduating high school.

His parents had given him a small check and said they were proud of him but their words had seemed empty to him. He could still remember the way his mother had looked at him, as if she thought he'd threatened the principal into giving him his diploma. His father had patted him on the back, awkward as always when any outward display of affection was required.

In a rare weak moment, Jake had said something to Pop about never being able to please them. He'd thought that getting his diploma would be something that would finally make them proud of him. He'd finally done something right. But it still wasn't enough. He went on to tell Pop that Frank's parents had driven all the way to Boise to take him out to dinner, while his own mother hadn't even bothered to bake him a cake.

Pop had told him not to whine but the next time Jake had dropped by for his self-defense lessons, there'd been a three-layer cake sitting on the counter in Pop's rarely used kitchen. A three-layer cake that was about an inch and a half high. Jake had manfully attempted to eat a slice—he wouldn't have hurt Pop's feelings for the world—but the cake was just the consistency of not quite hardened cement.

They'd ended the evening by going to Maisie's for a slice of apple pie after burying the cake with great ceremony. Jake shook his head. It was funny how the good memories had lingered while the reason they'd happened had all but been forgotten.

Pop peered up at him, his faded eyes searching Jake's face for answers. "You look like you've had some rough times, Jake. It's good to have you home, boy."

Emotion caught in Jake's throat. Here was the welcome he hadn't gotten from his parents. This old man had been about the only person in the entire town who'd believed in him, who'd believed he could make something of himself. He'd made something of himself all right, but he doubted it was what Pop had had in mind.

"Thanks, Pop." Jake squeezed the old man's shoulder. "I'll be seeing you around."

"I'll be here."

Pop settled back into his chair by the door and Jake moved toward the teller window. The clerk's eyes widened when she saw the size of the check he wanted to cash, but after making a call to the bank it was drawn on, she cashed it without protest. He'd considered opening an account but an inner voice had suggested that it would make things more difficult if he should decide to leave suddenly. Considering Pop was the only one who seemed genuinely glad to see him, that was a strong possibility.

He was tucking his wallet back into his pocket when he felt someone watching him. When he looked up, his gaze collided with that of a tall, dark-haired woman who was standing a few feet away. It had been twenty years but he didn't have any trouble recognizing her. She watched his approach much as she might have watched a cougar about to jump on its prey.

"Josie."

"Jake." She nodded, her eyes a cold brown. "I heard you were back in town."

"Doesn't look like the grapevine has withered any in the last twenty years."

She didn't bother to acknowledge his mild sarcasm. "Why are you here?"

"I was cashing a check," he said, knowing that wasn't what she'd been asking.

She made an impatient gesture with one manicured hand. "I don't mean that. I mean, why have you come back to Riverbend?"

"Is there any reason I shouldn't have come back?" He was getting just a little tired of answering the same question and his irritation showed in his tone.

"There doesn't seem to be any reason you'd want to come back."

"I don't recall being run out of town on a rail."

"Well, you've been gone nearly twenty years, Jake. You can't blame people for being a little surprised to see you."

"Maybe." He looked at her, searching for something of the girl he'd loved so passionately. There didn't seem to be any trace of her left in the rather cool woman standing in front of him. "How's Frank?"

"He's fine. Are you staying long?"

It didn't take a psychic to figure out that nothing would have made her happier than to hear that he was on his way out of town.

"I don't know. With the heartwarming welcome everyone has offered, it's a little difficult to think about leaving just yet."

Color mantled her cheeks but he didn't think it was out of embarrassment. Anger was a better bet.

"I really can't imagine that there's anything here for you, Jake."

"Can't you?" He allowed the silence to stretch.

The skin over Josie's cheeks seemed to tighten, the carefully concealed lines beside her eyes deepening. "I have to go."

Jake watched her abrupt departure, wondering why Josie should be so anxious to see him leave town. He hadn't expected her to be delighted to see him, but neither had he expected veiled hostility. He followed more slowly, waving to Pop on the way out.

He started toward the motorcycle, slowing when he saw the man looking at it. The tan sheriff's uniform identified him even before he turned around.

Martin Smith had been two years behind Jake in high school, not as big a gap in a town the size of Riverbend as it might have been in a larger place. Martin turned as Jake stopped in front of the bike. The hair that had been carrot-red twenty years ago had darkened to a more subdued shade and the stockiness that had tended to fat in high school had become solid muscle.

"Jake Quincannon." Martin held out his hand, his smile easy, his eyes watchful. "Figured this had to be yours. I know every other bike in town. Heard you were back."

"Martin. Pop told me you'd taken over his job."

"You haven't been in town long."

"I'd guess you know the exact moment I crossed the city limits." There was no rancor in Jake's words.

Martin laughed. "Probably pretty close. You've sure had the grapevine humming."

"The place hasn't changed," Jake muttered.

"That's the way people want it. You go away, and when you come back, everything is just the way you left it."

"Is that why you came back? Pop told me you were in the service."

"Yeah. I did two tours in 'Nam. When I got home, I thought this place would drive me crazy. It was like they'd never gotten out of the fifties. But there's a certain peace in it, too."

Jake couldn't argue with that. God knows, peace was something he hadn't found. Maybe that's what he was looking for.

While he and Martin were talking, an armored car pulled up in front of the bank. The guard got out of the car, two sacks of money carried casually at his sides. The bank manager met him in the lobby and the two stood talking for a moment before making their way farther into the bank, and then out of sight. Inside the door, Jake could see Pop sitting in his chair, watching the exchange without much interest.

"Friday's payroll for half the businesses in town," Martin commented, seeing where Jake's attention was focused.

"Doesn't look like there's much security around," Jake commented.

"I've mentioned that to Mr. Nathan a few times but he's too cheap to hire extra guards for the delivery. So,

I try to be around when the delivery is made." He shrugged. "I doubt there's much to worry about. They'd have to find the place before they could rob it."

Jake turned back to the sheriff. Security or the lack thereof wasn't his problem anymore. He didn't even have any money in the bank.

"You're staying at the old Cudahy place, I hear," Martin said.

Jake swung his leg over the big motorcycle, settling into the wide leather seat.

"Does everyone in town know what I had for dinner last night, too?" The edge of sarcasm was resoundingly clear.

Martin narrowed his eyes as if trying to remember something. "Pizza." He grinned at the startled look Jake threw him. "I know Paige. Gussied-up frozen pizza is her one culinary talent."

Jake shook his head, half grinning. He knocked the kickstand back before starting the engine. Martin lifted his hand as the Harley roared away from the curb. Jake returned the gesture, aware that the tension he'd felt since yesterday had eased.

Pop had been glad to see him and Martin didn't seem to have any problem with his presence in town. He couldn't say that Paige hadn't been welcoming but there was something about her— He broke the thought off, his mouth tightening beneath the thick dark mustache. He'd come home to try and figure out where he wanted to go with his life, as if coming back to where it had started would clarify things. The last thing he wanted to do was get involved with his landlady. It shouldn't be hard to keep a little distance between them.

It was an easy decision to make but not quite so easy to keep. Pulling the bike to a halt in front of the house, Jake snapped the kickstand into place absently, his attention on the big oak tree that spread its branches over the front yard.

Perched on a branch halfway up the tree was a calico kitten, his piteous wails telling a heartrending tale of woe. Balanced uneasily on the lowest branch was the landlady Jake had just decided to avoid.

That Paige was uneasy in her current position was clear from the way she clung to the trunk of the oak as if it was a lifeline. As he watched, she inched her fingers toward a higher branch. She was talking to the kitten. Jake couldn't hear what she was saying but he could hear the reassuring cadence of her voice. Not at all reassured, the kitten continued to yowl pathetically.

Jake crossed the yard to stand under the tree. From this vantage point, he had an excellent view of those endless legs and the snug fit of her shorts.

"You're going to fall," he said conversationally.

Startled, she turned to look down at him, nearly fulfilling his prediction as the sudden movement upset her careful balance. Jake held his breath as she teetered. But she regained her balance almost immediately.

"Harry is stuck," she said, as if this disclosure was part of an ongoing conversation.

"It's not going to do Harry any good if you kill yourself trying to get him down."

"I can't just leave him there."

"I'd guess that Harry will come down when he's good and ready."

"He's so little." Paige turned to look up at the kitten.

"He got himself up there, he can get himself down," Jake said heartlessly. "Let me give you a hand."

She wavered, clearly torn between the common sense of his words and the plight of the kitten. As if sensing that rescue might not be as forthcoming as he'd hoped, Harry raised his thin voice in a terrified yowl, confirming the desperation of his position.

"Listen to the poor little thing." Paige looked back down at Jake, her eyes full of concern. "I can't leave him up there. What if he falls?"

"I'll go up after him." Jake heard the words as if they came from someone else. He knew as well as Harry did that a cat up a tree can come down any time he wants to. Furthermore, he didn't even like cats. And he was long past the age for climbing trees.

He repeated these arguments to himself as he balanced on one branch and caught hold of another, pulling himself up into the huge oak. Harry watched him suspiciously from a branch that was just out of reach.

But it was another pair of green eyes that had gotten him into this situation. Eyes that had sparkled with gratitude when he said he'd undertake the rescue. Paige watched him from the ground and he was more conscious of that than he had any right to be.

"Come here, cat," he muttered, pulling himself up onto a branch just thick enough to support his weight. Harry edged back, letting out a piteous mew. The branch beneath him creaked in protest and Jake had a sudden vision of himself plummeting to his death on a front lawn in Idaho. For fifteen years he'd lived with the possibility of death as a constant companion. Wouldn't it be ironic if he died in his own hometown, trying to rescue a kitten who didn't need rescuing because he was trying to impress a woman he didn't want to get involved with?

"Come on, Harry," he coaxed in a soothing tone. What he really wanted to do was get his hands around that furry little neck. Harry edged just a little farther out on the branch, keeping up his pathetic cries, even as he tried to murder his would-be rescuer.

"Can you get him?" Paige called up. "He's a little shy sometimes."

Jake eyed the kitten, who eyed him back. Harry didn't look shy to him. Harry looked stubborn.

"Come here, you little pest." The words were said from between Jake's clenched teeth, which may have accounted for the cat's reluctance to obey the command.

Exasperated, Jake lunged upward, scooping the startled kitten from its perch with one hand and clutching at the tree for balance with the other. Harry wailed in fright, struggling wildly. But now that Jake had him, he had no intention of letting him go. He made his way back down the tree, one hand full of spitting, scratching kitten.

"You got him."

Though he knew he was being a fool, Jake felt suffused with the warmth of Paige's smile. Harry, no more content now that he was safely on the ground, fastened small but very sharp teeth into Jake's finger.

"Ouch, damn!" Jake dropped the furious kitten, who disappeared in an orange and black streak across the lawn.

"Are you hurt?" Paige caught his hand before he could deny any serious injury. "Oh, look what he did to your hand."

"It's no big deal." He would have pulled his hand away but Paige held it firmly.

"Come on into the house. I'll put some disinfectant on those. Cat bites can be nasty, you know."

Still holding his hand, she led him across the yard and onto the porch. Jake told himself that he was going along with her only because he didn't want to make an issue of retrieving his hand. Besides, the bite was beginning to sting like the devil.

Paige sat him in a chair in the kitchen and turned to the drawer where she kept her somewhat haphazard first-aid kit. She was vividly aware of Jake watching her. Her fingers felt clumsy as she fumbled in the drawer.

"I'm sorry Harry wasn't more grateful," she said, turning back to him with a tube of antiseptic cream held like a shield in front of her.

"I've never really thought of cats as being grateful creatures," Jake commented.

Paige crouched down in front of him, reaching for his hand, trying not to notice the warmth of his skin. "Harry was a stray when Lisa took him in. I don't think he trusts humans very much."

"You mean it isn't even your cat?"

"No. Harry belongs to the little girl who lives across the street."

"What was he doing in your tree?" Jake demanded, sounding vaguely indignant.

"Maybe he liked the looks of my tree better than the one at home." She finished dabbing the injury with ointment and glanced up. "You know, the trees are always greener on the other side of the street."

Jake gave her a pained look but she thought she caught a twitch of amusement at the corner of his mouth. "Maybe Harry just wanted to see if he could get me killed," he muttered.

"It was really nice of you to go up after him," she said distractedly. It was funny how with only one eye, his gaze managed to be so penetrating. She'd forgotten she was holding his hand. She was suddenly aware of the intimacy of her position, crouched on the floor between his knees.

"No problem. Climbing into trees after cats that don't need rescuing is my speciality." Jake's gaze was on her mouth as he spoke. He lifted his free hand to take hold of the pale braid that hung over her shoulder. "I didn't remember how light your hair was—the color of sunlight."

Paige moistened her lips, aware of a sudden catch in her breath. She really should get up, she thought absently. But she didn't move. Jake's hand moved to the nape of her neck. The feel of his fingers resting on the sensitive skin there sent a tingling sensation up her spine.

She was hardly aware of releasing his hand as he pulled her upward. But she was vividly aware of the feel of his chest beneath her palms. As his face filled her vision, she closed her eyes.

His mouth was firm and warm. The brush of his mustache against her upper lip was a sensuous tickle. She edged closer as his hands splayed against her upper back. The kiss was slow, almost lazy. His mouth explored hers without urgency.

Jake hadn't planned on kissing her. But her mouth had looked so soft, so inviting. A small kiss, he told himself. No big deal, nothing to even really think about. But he hadn't planned on the way the kiss seemed to take on a life of its own. He'd thought that, if he kissed her, he'd be able to stop wondering what her mouth would taste like. Instead, he found himself wanting to draw her closer, to see if her skin could possibly be as soft as it looked.

Paige had experienced more passionate kisses but she'd never experienced a kiss that seemed to plunge right into her soul. When Jake lifted his head, she could only stare at him. His look was searching, as if the simple kiss had been more than he'd expected, too.

If he released her, would she melt into a puddle, just like the Wicked Witch of the West? It seemed a distinct possibility. The thought was enough to force strength back into her spine.

"Well, I've heard of kissing it to make it better but I thought *I* was the one who was supposed to kiss your injury." Her voice was a little too husky but it was steady, the tone just light enough.

Jake's hands slid from her back and she scooted back before standing up.

"Consider it a thank-you for my rescuing Harry," Jake said, rising from the chair. He didn't seem in the least disturbed by the kiss, she noted, feeling an odd twinge of irritation.

"In that case, maybe you should have kissed Harry."

Halfway out the door, Jake turned, raking her with a look of pure masculine appreciation. "Harry isn't nearly as pretty."

Paige stood in the middle of the kitchen floor, listening to the thumping of his feet as he took the stairs two at a time. She had the feeling that Jake Quincannon was going to shake up a lot of things in Riverbend this summer. If her accelerated pulse was any indication, she didn't think her own life was going to be immune, either.

The thought was not without appeal.

Chapter Four

"Okay, give me all the juicy details."

Mary's piercing whisper very probably reached every corner of the library. Early weekday afternoons were generally slow, so there was no one in the library to frown at Mary for disturbing the silence.

Paige had been returning books to the shelves but she'd stopped to peruse a book of poetry. She shut the book as she turned to look at her friend.

"Juicy details about what?"

"About Jake Quincannon," Mary whispered, her dark eyes sparkling with anticipation.

"There's really not much to tell." Paige turned to slip the book back onto the shelf. It might as well have been a treatise on nuclear physics. She hadn't really registered much of what she'd been reading. In fact, she hadn't been able to concentrate on anything today. But it certainly didn't have anything to do with her boarder. And nothing at all to do with that brief kiss they'd shared.

"Paige Cudahy, don't you dare clam up on me. Martin won't tell me a thing. You'd think it was a state secret or something."

"Maybe Martin thinks Jake wouldn't appreciate being front-page news," Paige said.

"Then he shouldn't have come back to Riverbend," Mary responded with irrefutable logic.

"What did Martin say?" Paige picked up the small stack of books she was supposed to be reshelving.

"Don't think I don't know that you're trying to avoid answering the question, Paige." Mary trailed along after her friend, her quick movements making it seem as if she was taking two steps for every one of Paige's. "All Martin would say is that Jake seemed like a nice guy. A nice guy! What kind of description is that? I could have strangled him."

"Strangling him would probably have jeopardized your wedding plans." Paige slipped a volume onto the shelf.

"I suppose. Sometimes I don't know why I agreed to marry him."

"Because you're madly in love with him and he's madly in love with you."

"That's true." Mary held out her left hand, admiring the way the small diamond on her third finger caught the sunlight that poured in through the front windows.

"But that doesn't change the fact that he's the most exasperating man in the world," she said, hurrying to catch up with Paige, who'd moved down one of the stacks.

"All men are exasperating."

"You're not doing too badly yourself." Mary took Paige's arm in a determined grip. "I want to know all about Jake Quincannon."

"You've come to the wrong source. I hardly know him."

"Paige."

How someone so short could inject so much threat into one word was something Paige couldn't understand. But she knew that look. Mary wasn't going to budge until she'd pried every detail from her victim.

"If you're going to pump me for information, I might as well be comfortable while you're doing it."

Sighing in defeat, Paige made her way to the desk and collapsed back into the huge chair she'd convinced the library committee was absolutely essential to a librarian's comfort. Mary perched on the edge of the desk, crossing her jeans-clad legs at the ankle.

"Okay, tell me everything. What does he look like?"

"Actually, I guess he looks pretty much like a returning rebel should look. Dark hair, with just a touch of gray at the temples. Black mustache, very ominous-looking. And blue eyes, at least the one you can see is blue. He wears a patch over the left eye."

"I told Sally Ann Hartford I didn't believe her when she told me he wore an eye patch." Mary sounded guilt stricken.

"I wouldn't worry about it. It's probably the first time Sally's told the truth in the last five years. It's not your fault you didn't believe her."

Mary dismissed the mendacious Sally with a wave of her hand. "She doesn't like me anyway." She leaned forward, her dark eyes bright. "What's he like, Paige? Is he lean and hungry, or sullen? Does he send shivers up your spine?"

Paige devoted her attention to picking an invisible piece of lint from her skirt, her eyes focused on the task. Shivers up her spine? She had to admit that he did, though not in the way Mary meant. But that was something she'd decided not to think about, at least not right now.

"He's definitely not sullen," she told her friend. "And he's too big to be lean and hungry. He seems nice."

"Nice?" Mary repeated the word disappointedly. She'd been hoping for something a little more provocative than "nice." "Is that all? Just 'nice'?"

"A little lonely maybe."

"Why did he come back to Riverbend? Miss Leigh, over at the post office, says that he's sent postcards from all over the world to his parents. If he's been all over the world, why would he want to come back here?"

"Maybe he just got tired of traveling," Paige suggested, remembering how he'd told her that he'd come back because he was looking for something. "Maybe he wanted to see his parents."

"I suppose." Mary sighed, looking as disconsolate as her sunny personality would allow. "I was really hoping he'd stir things up a bit. Nothing awful, just something to add a little spice to the summer. I thought maybe I'd get some ideas for my next book."

"What happened to the one about the knife thrower who's also a spy?"

"I just got it back in the mail. They said it didn't ring true," Mary said indignantly. "After all the research on circuses I did. And they said it was too long. I needed every one of those pages for plot development."

Paige offered commiserations, controlling the urge to comment that eight hundred pages of plot development was enough to exhaust anybody.

Mary turned to glance over her shoulder as the big wooden door that fronted Oakwood Street was thrust open. It banged back against the wall and Paige made a mental note to talk to the library committee about that. Of course, most of the patrons were familiar with the door's idiosyncrasies and avoided throwing it open. But then most of the patrons weren't Josie.

Josie never just walked through a door. There had been a time when Paige had despaired of ever being able to enter a room like her older sister, so that all eyes immediately turned her way. She'd long ago stopped trying to emulate Josie's entrances or anything else about her, but she still felt a twinge of admiration as she watched her sister sweep into the small library. Her heels clicked on the old wooden floor, sending out an almost military tattoo that demanded attention.

"Oh-oh. It's Morgana le Fey," Mary muttered as she slid off the desk and turned to face Josie, who had just swept up to the desk.

"Hello, Josie. I like that suit." Paige tried to defuse the anger she could see simmering in Josie's eyes. The diversion worked only for a moment.

"It was a gift from Frank. Chanel, you know."

She spoke condescendingly, and Paige saw Mary's hand twitch with the urge to smack Josie. It was an urge Josie brought out in a number of people. Paige didn't know how to explain that Josie didn't mean to be insulting. She felt she was so clearly superior to nearly everyone in town that it never occurred to her that anyone would be insulted by anything she said or did.

Not that she'd have cared much if they were insulted, Paige admitted to herself.

"Chanel?" Paige spoke quickly, forestalling anything Mary might be about to say. "Frank must have sold a house."

Josie's husband was an attorney by profession, but because Riverbend wasn't big enough to require a full-time attorney, he also handled most of the real estate deals that came up.

"Yes, he did. Over in Banning. You know, if you weren't so stubborn, Paige, he could take that old white elephant off your hands. You could get a smaller place, something modern and efficient."

"Sorry." She wasn't really sorry but there was no sense in telling her sister that.

"Really. I don't know why Mom and Dad left the house to you in the first place. *I* grew up there, too, you know."

"And it obviously holds great sentimental value for you," Mary commented sweetly.

"Of course it does," Josie said, oblivious of her own insincerity. "But I understand property values in a way you obviously don't, Paige. The place has gone up considerably in value. If you sold now, you could make a nice profit."

"And Frank could buy you another mink," Mary said, without trying to hide the sarcasm.

"Actually, we've been discussing the fact that Beth needs a car." There was a faint air of maternal martyrdom in her tone. Paige was well aware that Josie was hoping that the idea of being instrumental in getting her niece a car was supposed to weaken her refusal. She leaned back in the chair, careful to keep the amusement from her expression. Josie was so transparent sometimes.

"I'm not interested in selling, Josie. Frank knows that and he seems to understand."

"Frank's just not firm enough," Josie said irritably.

"I can think of a few places he might have applied a firmer hand," Mary said sweetly.

Josie blinked, apparently surprised to see that Mary was still there. She frowned for a moment, as if trying to decipher Mary's meaning and then, with a toss of her head, she dismissed it as being of no importance. She returned her attention to Paige—and to the subject that had brought her to the library in the first place.

"I suppose you've heard that Jake Quincannon is back in town."

"Yes." Paige made the admission cautiously. Josie obviously didn't know that Paige had rented Jake a room, though how the grapevine had missed spreading that juicy tidbit, she couldn't imagine.

"I saw him yesterday at the bank."

"Really." Monosyllables were generally the safest way of responding to Josie's questions. Why hadn't Jake mentioned that he'd seen Josie?

"Arrogant bastard." Paige was startled by the venom in Josie's tone. She hadn't expected her sister to be thrilled with Jake's return, but there didn't seem to be any real reason for such hostility.

"What did he do?"

"Nothing." Josie spit the word out as if it were a condemnation. "He just looked at me. He was wearing a hideous eye patch. It made my skin crawl just to look at it."

"The man can't help it if he lost an eye, Josie." Paige's voice held a sharp note that, as usual, Josie didn't hear.

"He probably doesn't even need it. It would be just like him to put a patch over his eye just for effect." Josie tugged petulantly at the bottom of her jacket.

"I don't remember Jake going out of his way to impress people," Paige said, wondering, not for the first time, if it was possible that she'd been adopted. Sometimes it seemed unlikely that she and Josie were related by blood.

"What would you know?" Josie snapped. "You were just a fat little girl who always had her nose in a book."

Mary drew in a sharp breath and Paige grabbed hold of the back of her shirt, giving it a warning tug. She didn't need Mary leaping to her defense.

"Why should you care whether or not Jake is back, Josie? He's probably here to see his parents."

"Well, they aren't going to be any happier to see him than anyone else is. They never did like him." There was a certain smug satisfaction in Josie's voice. Thinking of the lonely boy she remembered from twenty years ago, Paige felt a rare urge toward physical violence.

"Anyway, I don't care," Josie said. "I just think it's a shame he came back. I thought I ought to warn you that he was in town. If you take my advice, you'll avoid him. Not that he's likely to have any interest in you," she added with casual cruelty. "I doubt if he'd even remember you."

"Probably not," Paige said, keeping a firm grip on Mary's shirt.

"Well, I have to go. I've a committee meeting this afternoon." Josie glanced around the library, her mouth pursed in a moue of distaste. "I don't know how you can stand this place, Paige. It's so gloomy."

"Libraries are supposed to be gloomy, Josie. It's a tradition."

"I suppose. You know, it's too bad you didn't finish your degree. If you'd stuck with it long enough to get a teaching certificate, you wouldn't have had to take a job like this."

Paige tugged so fiercely on Mary's shirt that the collar cut off her breath, preventing the anger inside her from exploding.

"It is too bad." Paige left it to Josie to decide just what was too bad.

"Now, don't forget what I said about Jake, Paige. I know how you tend to feel sorry for everyone, but Jake Quincannon is not one of your interminable stream of stray dogs."

Josie swept out on a wave of Giorgio, banging the door back against the wall as she left.

Paige relaxed her grip on Mary's shirt, well aware that an explosion was inevitable. Mary didn't disappoint her. She turned, her round face flushed, her eyes fairly snapping with anger.

"That...that...bitch!" She stuttered with rage. "I'm sorry, Paige. I know she's your sister but she's really the most selfish, insensitive, stupid cow I've ever had the misfortune to meet."

"You can't really say Josie's a cow, Mary." Paige made the correction blandly. "You can't be a size eight and a cow at the same time."

"How do you stand her?" Mary paced back and forth in front of the desk.

"I don't see all that much of her."

"How dare she make nasty remarks about you not getting your degree. I suppose she doesn't remember that if you hadn't come home after your mother's stroke, there wouldn't have been anyone to take care of her. Josie certainly had no intention of doing it."

"Josie already had a husband and child to take care of." It was a discussion they'd had before and Paige saw no reason to go over it again. She stood up and stretched, aware of the knot of tension that had settled in the back of her neck. It didn't seem to matter that she understood her sister backward and forward. It didn't even help that Josie's single-minded devotion to herself was so exaggerated that it was amusing. Spending any time at all in Josie's presence still made her feel tense.

She half listened as Mary enumerated Josie's faults. She wondered vaguely if she should say something in her sister's defense but she doubted if she could manage it with any sincerity. It was unfortunate, but true, that Josie really was one of the most unlikable people she'd ever known.

The rest of the afternoon passed in welcome quiet. The citizens of Riverbend were proud of their library, but they didn't make much use of it. She was able to lock the big front door a little after five, drawing in a deep breath of warm air. The sun was slipping behind the mountains to the west, but daylight would linger for another hour or so.

Paige waved to several people as she walked home, but she didn't stop to talk to anyone. She wasn't in the mood for idle chitchat this evening, especially when the topic was almost certain to be her new boarder.

JAKE TAPPED THE HAMMER against the nail, coaxing it into the wood. The thin slats didn't require much force. He sat back on his heels, looking at the old swing with a critical eye. Not bad really, he decided. No one was likely to call on him to build a house but the porch swing was certainly in better shape than it had been. He hadn't planned on fixing it, but the sagging seat had caught his eye.

He arched his shoulders back, aware of a not unpleasant ache. Weighing the hammer in his hand, he grinned to himself, pleased with the results of his afternoon's work.

"It won't do, you know."

He stood up and turned. Paige was looking at him from the bottom of the steps, her head tilted to one side. Her hair fell over her shoulder in that thick braid that made his fingers itch to undo it. She was wearing a slim skirt that revealed a tantalizing length of leg and a tailored blouse in a shade that hovered between blue and green.

"What won't do?" He was no longer surprised by the way she always started conversations in the middle.

"You." She gestured to the hammer as she walked up the steps. "You look far too domestic. Not at all the image everyone expects you to project."

"Since there was no one around, I didn't think I'd put too many dents in my reputation."

"That shows how much you've forgotten about this town." She nodded toward the big yellow house across the street. "Mrs. McCardle's curtain is twitching so hard, it's a wonder it hasn't come off the rod. And Mr. Dumphy hasn't taken a pair of shears to that hedge in ten years."

Jake turned to look at the old man two doors down who suddenly seemed terribly interested in his hedge. When his eyes shifted to the window across the street, the plain white curtain gave a convulsive heave and then was still.

"That was not protocol," Paige said, as she slipped off her shoes, kicking them in the general direction of the front door. "You're not supposed to notice them."

"But it's all right for them to keep an eye on me?"

He arched one brow as she sank onto the newly repaired swing.

"Of course. Everyone has his place in Riverbend. Some people are watchers and others are watchees."

"Watchees?" Jake's mouth twitched in a smile. "There is no such word."

"There is now. You are a *watchee*. You're supposed to go around giving the *watchers* something to watch. Repairing my porch swing isn't what they've got in mind. But I appreciate it anyway." She stretched her legs out, propping her feet on an empty wicker planter that had once been white but had long since faded to a dusty gray. She leaned her head back and closed her eyes, apparently ready for a nap.

"I hope you don't mind," he said, with just a touch of sarcasm. "I should have asked before taking a hammer to your house, but I had some time on my hands and the swing looked a little rickety."

"You don't have to be polite, Jake," she said without opening her eyes. "The swing was falling to pieces. I should have had it taken down years ago. But I'm glad I didn't. I'd forgotten how comfortable it was. Why don't you try it out?"

She patted the seat beside her. Jake hesitated. He'd already decided that getting involved with Paige would be a big mistake. In fact, he'd made up his mind to do no such thing. But sitting with her wasn't really getting involved.

He stepped over her legs and settled gingerly onto the seat next to her. She didn't move or speak, and Jake gradually relaxed back against the curved wooden slats. Somewhere on the next block, he could hear the shouts of children at play.

A bee buzzed lazily around a fat rose blossom that nodded over the porch railing. Watching it, Jake realized that *this* was the reason he'd come back here. Lazy summer afternoons with twilight creeping in from the mountains. Nothing to think about except what to have for dinner.

Peace. More than anything in the world, he'd come home looking for peace. He let his eyes drift shut, unconsciously pushing one foot against the plank floor to set the swing into gentle motion.

He'd spent two decades traveling around the world, learning to live with danger the way another man might live with a nagging wife. Always, in the back of his mind, had been the thought that there was something missing in his life.

It wasn't the stability of a home life exactly. He wasn't looking for a white picket fence and a lawn to mow. He'd had that growing up and he'd learned that it wasn't a magic cure-all.

After losing his eye, he'd had time to think and he'd realized that what was missing was a certain inner peace, an acceptance of himself, of what he'd been and what he was now. That's what he'd come home to find.

He had no idea how long they'd been sitting there when Paige broke the silence.

"Jake?"

"Hmm?"

"Why did you fix the swing?"

He didn't move but there was a shrug in his voice. "It's been a long time since I did anything constructive with my hands. I guess I just wanted to see if I could. Besides, I used to love this swing."

"Because it reminds you of Josie?"

"Not particularly. When I'd come to pick her up for a date, she was never ready. Your mother would answer the door and tell me that Josie would be down in a minute. I always sat on this swing while I was waiting. I dreamed a lot of dreams on this swing."

"Did any of them come true?" There was a wistful note in the question and he turned his head, looking at her profile.

"Some of them," he said, after a moment, thinking of how he'd always wanted to see the world. He'd done that, though it hadn't been quite the way he'd dreamed.

"I'm glad," she said simply.

"What about you? Have you done what you've dreamed of?"

She opened her eyes, rolling her head toward him. "Does anyone dream of being a librarian in the town where she was born?"

There was a note in her voice he couldn't quite place. Not sarcasm or bitterness. More a rueful acknowledgment that life hadn't turned out quite the way she'd planned.

"Librarian? I pictured you running some chic little boutique."

"In Riverbend?" She laughed, a husky sound that seemed to slide down his spine. "I don't think this town is ready for chic boutiques just yet. Besides, being the town's one and only librarian carries a certain cachet that merely running a store couldn't possibly match. *I* am invited to the meetings of the Library Committee, the Committee to Improve Young Minds *and* the Mayor's Committee for the Betterment of the Community.''

Jake blinked. "I'm impressed."

"Don't be. I'm not." Her smile took any sarcasm out of the words. "Actually, it's not a bad job. The library is only open a few hours a day and we're closed Sundays and Wednesdays. It doesn't do a booming business, so there aren't any real demands on my time. The library committee is grateful to have someone with half an English degree, and it gives me something to do. Besides, now I can read all I want and no one ever tells me to get my nose out of a book or that all that reading is going to do for me is make me crosseyed.''

"Is that what people told you when you were little?"

"Constantly." She watched as the bee abandoned the rose, buzzing importantly off toward the hive. "Not that I blame them. If I was awake, I was probably reading. Actually, it's a wonder I'm not crosseyed.''

"Your eyes look fine to me," Jake said, responding to the almost imperceptible note of recollected hurt.

"Thank you." She shifted, tucking her feet up under her as she turned to look him squarely in the face. "You know, you're really rather nice, despite that gruff exterior."

Jake drew back, emotionally as well as physically. Her casual honesty was both appealing and threatening. One thing he was learning about Paige Cudahy was that she didn't seem to see the barriers the rest of the world found so apparent.

"Don't you like being called nice?" she asked, sensing his withdrawal.

When she put it that way, feeling threatened by her compliment seemed ridiculous. It wasn't that he didn't *like* it. He just didn't know how to respond to it.

"I don't really mind," he said cautiously.

"I promise not to tell anyone else," she offered.

She was teasing him again. He could hear it in her voice and see it in the way her eyes seemed to be laughing at him. He stifled a sudden urge to pull her into his arms and kiss her until that hint of laughter darkened into passion.

"I'm not worried. No one would believe you anyway, so I don't think my reputation would be threatened."

"We can still keep it our little secret."

She made the offer so solemnly that Jake felt a smile tugging at his mouth again. He reached out and took hold of the thick braid that lay over her shoulder, giving it a quick tug.

"You know, I seem to recall that you were a bit of a brat when you pulled your nose out of that book you seemed to have with you all the time. You haven't changed."

"Thank you," she said demurely.

Jake laughed, the sound rusty from lack of use. Leaning back in a corner of the swing, he could feel years of tension flowing out of him.

Chapter Five

Jake eased the Harley to a stop. He took his time putting the kickstand into place, half wishing he could change his mind about this visit. But it was too late. His father had been watering the flower beds that lined the porch, but he turned at the sound of the Harley, watching as Jake swung his leg over the bike and started up the brick path.

"Hello, Jake." His weathered face eased into a cautious smile, his eyes watchful.

"Hi, Dad." Jake walked up the pathway until he stood beside his father. "The roses look great this year."

"I've got a few prizewinners in there." There was pride in his father's voice and Jake felt a sudden twinge of old pain. Twenty years ago, he'd have given his soul to hear that same note of pride turned toward him. But then, he hadn't really given his father much to be proud of, if the truth were told.

The silence stretched, threatening to become awkward. Staring at the fleeting rainbow patterns in the spray of water, Jake groped for something to say. Why was it so difficult? After all, this was his father, his family.

"I think you grew a bit after you left home, boy."
It was obvious that his father was struggling as much
as he was to keep the conversation going. Well, at least
they had something in common, Jake thought with a
touch of sardonic humor.

"You look the same," he lied.

"Well, the hair's a little grayer, I'd guess."

"Mine too," Jake said dryly.

His father looked at him in surprise, really looking
at him for the first time, seeing the gray at his temples, the lines that experience had drawn beside his
eyes.

"I guess I tend to forget that you're a grown man
now, Jake. You weren't much more than a boy when
you left home."

"A boy with a chip on his shoulder," Jake admitted, half smiling.

"Well, I reckon most of us have had a bit too much
pride, one time or another."

Jake returned his father's smile, feeling as if the wall
that Time had put between them shrank just a little.
They'd never been close but there'd been fleeting moments of understanding. If they could recapture even
that much, this trip wouldn't have been wasted.

"Lawrence, you're going to drown those roses of
yours." His mother's voice preceded her out of the
dim front hallway. The disembodied sound shattered
the moment like a hammer on glass. Jake's father
turned away, twisting the nozzle to stop the flow of
water. Jake's smile vanished.

Margaret had pushed open the screen door and
stepped onto the shady porch before she saw her son.
The lines around her eyes seemed to tighten and
deepen. "Jacob. I didn't realize you were here."

"Hello, Mother." Jake reached up to check the black leather patch, as if the gesture might somehow make it less noticeable. "I hope this isn't a bad time."

"Of course not." There was no emotion in her voice. She could have been talking to the mailman, though Jake suspected there might have been more welcome in it. "You're family. You're welcome anytime."

The words might have sounded more sincere if they hadn't been uttered in such a flat tone. Jake shoved his hands into his back pockets, wondering how you started repairing a twenty-year-old breach. No, come to think of it, there'd never been a time when he and his mother hadn't been at odds with each other.

"Thank you, Mother."

"You don't have to thank me, Jake. It's only what's right."

"And you always do what's right, don't you?"

"I try." If she heard the bitterness in his voice, she chose to ignore it. "Trying to do what's right is a Christian's duty, Jacob. It's what the good Lord asks of us."

"It seems to me there's also something in the Bible about loving your children."

"And a commandment to honor thy father and mother, Jacob," she shot back, her gray eyes suddenly flaring with emotion.

"Touché, Mother." Jake acknowledged the hit with a mocking lift of his eyebrow.

"Lunch is almost ready, isn't it, Mother?" Lawrence stepped between the two of them, literally and figuratively. "Why don't you join us, Jake? Mother made one of her potpies. Best in the county."

Jake hesitated. His first urge was to turn and walk away. But his father's eyes held a look that could almost have been a plea. He'd spent the first twenty years of his life walking away from his problems with his mother; it hadn't solved anything then and it wouldn't solve anything now.

"I'd like that, Dad. If it wouldn't be an inconvenience..." He looked up at his mother where she still stood on the porch.

"I've already said you're welcome here, Jacob." There was not a flicker of expression in her eyes. "If you're staying to lunch, you'll want to wash your hands."

Ten minutes later, Jake seated himself at the sturdy oak table that had sat in the corner of his mother's kitchen for as long as he could remember. A blue and white checked cloth covered the table, a fitting backdrop for the plain white dishes. The room was cozy and homey. The rich scent of chicken potpie filled the big kitchen. The scene was right out of a magazine article on country living.

But Jake didn't feel particularly cozy and he didn't feel at home. He bowed his head while his father murmured a blessing, struggling against the feeling of having fallen into a time warp. He had to keep reminding himself that he wasn't sixteen anymore. He was an adult, able to meet his parents on equal ground. He'd made his own way in the world.

"Pass the salt, please, Jake."

Jake reached for the white porcelain saltshaker in answer to his father's request.

"Now you know the doctor told you to stay away from salt, Lawrence."

"Doc Burnett is an old fussbudget." Lawrence liberally dusted the steaming potpie.

"Well, it's your decision, of course," Margaret said disapprovingly. "But you'll have no one to blame but yourself if your blood pressure goes even higher than it already is."

"Do you have a problem with your blood pressure, Dad?"

"It's nothing serious, Jake." Lawrence brushed his concern away. "Like I said, Doc Burnett likes to fuss."

"And I suppose that's why he's got you taking those pills and that's why he has you in for a checkup every few months," Margaret said tartly.

"I wish I'd known, Dad," Jake said with concern.

"There's nothing to know," Lawrence said. "I'm as healthy as a horse."

"If you'd come home a little more often than once every twenty years, Jacob, you *would* have known."

Jake's fingers tightened on his fork. "It's not as if I had dropped off the face of the earth, Mother. I did write."

"Postcards two or three times a year." She sniffed her contempt.

"I don't think you did much better. Most years, all I got from you was a note in a Christmas card."

"Can't the two of you stop your fighting for just one meal?" Lawrence asked in exasperation. "I swear, you argued for twenty years and now you're picking up just where you left off."

His words put an end to any conversation for several minutes. Jake ate his meal doggedly, without tasting it. His mother had put a glass of milk out for him, he noticed. Just as if he were still ten years old.

He wondered what she'd do if he asked for a beer instead, but there was no sense in baiting her.

The milk made him think of his first night home. Paige had offered him milk in a Tweety Bird glass. He wondered what she'd think of this tense, silent meal. She'd probably tell him that it was his fault. And she would probably be right, he admitted grudgingly. He had to take at least a portion of the blame for the fact that he and his mother had never gotten along.

He hadn't come home to renew old problems. If anything, he'd come back to resolve them. And he might as well start here and now. He drew in a breath, forcing his face into what he hoped was a pleasant expression.

"It doesn't look like the town has changed much," he said to no one in particular.

"No, that it hasn't," Lawrence said, relieved to have the silence broken. "That it hasn't."

"Some people don't see much reason for change just for the sake of change," Margaret said, without looking up from her meal. "Most of us like Riverbend just the way it is."

"No reason you shouldn't," Jake said, determined to ignore the challenge in her voice. "It's a nice little town."

"With all the places you've been, I'd think Riverbend might seem a little dull," she said, dabbing at her mouth with a snow-white cloth napkin. "I wouldn't think there'd be much for you to do here."

"You've said that before, Mother." His voice sounded forced and he stopped, trying to relax. "I'm sure I'll find enough to do."

She put down the napkin, fixing him with a cool stare. Jake remembered that look from his childhood. It usually meant she was about to tell him to comb his hair or wash his face, always in that coolly critical tone that made him feel as if he'd failed some important test.

"Why *did* you come back here, Jacob?"

"Why does everyone keep asking me that?" He put his fork down, setting his hands on the edge of the table. "Other people have left town and then come back. Everyone acts like I robbed the bank and was sent off to prison."

"If it hadn't been for Joe Bellows thinking you could do no wrong, that's exactly where you would have ended up," she said harshly.

"Now, Mother," Lawrence put his hand on his wife's arm. "That's not rightly true. Jake never did anything harmful."

"Except that I didn't die when Michael did."

Margaret drew in a shocked breath, the color draining from her face. For a moment, the silence was so intense, it seemed like a fourth party in the room. Jake's gaze was locked with his mother's. He could read the struggle there as anger fought with her habitual control.

Her slim hand was clenched on the edge of the table and he knew she was controlling the urge to slap him. He almost wished she would, that just once, she'd let go and give him something real to combat.

"I think you should apologize to your mother, Jake." Lawrence's tone was stern. "She's never wished that you'd died when your brother did. That was all a long time ago and there's no sense in bringing it up now."

The words broke the tension. Margaret lowered her eyes, her hand slowly relaxing on the edge of the table. Jake knew there'd be no explosion and no discussion. He didn't offer an apology, but it wasn't really expected. The little incident was over, filed away as unfinished business, just as all such incidents had been during his childhood.

"You must admit, Jacob, that it's a little strange that you should come home after twenty years of gallivanting all over the world." Margaret picked up the conversation, as if the brief digression had never occurred. She stood up, picked up her plate and her husband's and carried them to the sink.

"Gallivanting can be tiring." Jake pushed his plate away. The few bites he'd eaten couldn't account for the knot in his stomach. He was beginning to wonder, along with everyone else, just why he'd come home.

The knock on the back door was a welcome interruption. The door had been left open to allow the light breeze to drift through the house. The visitor was visible only as a silhouette through the screen door.

"Hi, thought I'd drop by to see if there was anything you needed." The sentence was punctuated by the creak of the door being pulled open, as the newcomer, clearly feeling very much at home, didn't bother to wait for an invitation.

Jake shoved his chair back from the table and stood, feeling a new surge of tension enter the room. Frank Hudson stopped dead when he saw Jake, his expression startled.

There had been a time when he and Jake had been as close as brothers. They'd grown up together, shared their dreams and ambitions. But that had been a long time ago. The last time they'd met had been when Jake came home to find that Frank had married Josie. They'd fought bitterly. Jake had taken away a split lip, a black eye and what he'd then believed was a broken heart. He'd left Frank with a broken nose, a few loose teeth and the girl he'd thought was his.

They were both a lot older now, with any luck a lot wiser. Frank hadn't changed much. His sandy-brown hair had thinned a bit and he'd gotten a little soft around the middle. He'd never been handsome but there'd always been a warmth about him, a friendliness that drew people to him. When they were growing up, he'd had more friends than Jake could count. Jake had had only Frank. At the time, it had seemed enough.

"Frank." Jake nodded, his expression watchful. His fingers curled as he resisted the urge to make sure the patch was safely in place.

"Jake. I heard you were back in town."

"The grapevine has Western Union beat all to hell."

"It always did," Frank said, smiling. He stepped forward, extending his hand. "How are you?"

"I'm okay. And you?" Jake shook his hand, feeling the tension in the room ease. Out the corner of his eye, he could see his father relax back into his chair. What had they expected? That he'd go for Frank's throat?

"I can't complain," Frank said. "Josie said she saw you yesterday."

Jake would have bet any amount of money that Josie had had considerably more to say than just that she'd seen him. But there was no reason to bring that up.

"We ran into each other at the bank," he said nonchalantly. "I met Beth the morning after I got home. She seems like a great kid. You must be proud of her."

Was it his imagination or was the tension suddenly back with a vengeance?

"I am." If the atmosphere had changed, Frank didn't seem to have noticed it. "How long do you think you'll stay?"

Jake shrugged. "My plans are loose. Maybe for the summer, maybe less. What are you doing these days?"

"I got my law degree and I do a fair business."

"Sounds good. Lawyers are always in demand.

"I make out. Thanks, Mrs. Quincannon." Frank turned to take a cup of coffee from Jake's mother.

"Frank is real successful," she said, looking at Jake as if expecting him to disagree. "He's head of the chamber of commerce. He'll probably be mayor in a few more years. People look up to him."

"Oh, I don't know about that." Frank shook his head, clearly embarrassed by her words.

"They do so, Frank Hudson, and you know it." There was a wealth of affection both in her tone and in the way she looked at him. Jake tried to remember if she'd ever looked at him that way. If she had, he couldn't recall it. Maybe he should have joined the chamber of commerce.

"I've got to be going," he said abruptly.

"Don't go on my account," Frank said, looking concerned. "I can't stay."

"Frank comes by to see us real often," Margaret told Jake pointedly. "He's been a real help to us."

Implicit was the fact that Jake had not been a help. Frank flushed, clearly uneasy.

"Thank you for the meal, Mother. It was delicious," Jake said, carefully avoiding the conflict she seemed to be looking for.

"You didn't eat enough to tell one way or another," she said, moving past him to pick up his plate. There was a plea in his father's eyes that made Jake swallow the words hovering on the tip of his tongue.

He managed to say his farewells without further incident, escaping the house with the feeling that he was escaping a prison. He settled into the leather seat of the Harley and started it up. The afternoon stretched ahead of him. It was funny. He'd come home after all these years and now, three days into his stay, there wasn't anywhere he wanted to go or anyone he wanted to see. No one who'd be particularly glad to see him. The thought came back to him; maybe you really couldn't go home again.

"How could you do this to me, Paige?" Josie leaned one hand on the oak desk, looming over it like a lawyer demanding an answer from a particularly difficult witness.

"I don't see that I've done anything to you, Josie," Paige said calmly. "All I've done is rent Jake a room."

"*All* you've done?" Josie's voice rose. Heads turned, not even bothering to hide their interest in the little drama unfolding at the front of the library.

It was odd how the fact that she'd rented a room to Jake Quincannon had suddenly made the library a popular place. People who hadn't been near the library in years had suddenly taken a new interest in reading. And while they were there, there was certainly no harm in asking the librarian about her new boarder.

Paige's answers had been disappointingly vague, and the curious had generally left with a book tucked under their arms and with no more information than they'd come in with. Josie was certainly providing a lucky few with plenty to watch.

"Keep your voice down, Josie," Mary told her angrily. She'd arrived at the library before noon and had stayed glued to Paige's side with a loyalty that was deeply appreciated by her friend.

"Don't talk to me in that tone," Josie said, turning the full weight of her fury on Mary. Mary was unimpressed.

"Don't talk to Paige like that. It's none of your business what she does."

"Stop it. Both of you." Paige stood up, more irritated than angry.

"I don't see how you could do this, Paige. Have you no sense of loyalty?" Josie's tragic voice was worthy of a Sarah Bernhardt but it failed to visibly impress her sister.

"I don't see what the problem is, Josie. If I hadn't rented Jake a room, he'd just have found somewhere else to stay."

"That's no excuse." Josie dismissed the irrefutable logic of Paige's argument with a wave of her hand.

"I don't need an excuse. He wanted to rent a room. I had a room to rent. Plain and simple."

"It's not plain and simple," Josie said, in a whisper that could probably be heard in every corner of the room. "I don't want that man in my house."

"*Your* house?" Paige raised her eyebrows, her tone ominous.

"You know what I mean. It used to be my house. It should have been my house." She tugged petulantly at the narrow strap of her purse. "But that's not the point."

"Then why don't you get to the point, Josie? What *is* the problem with my renting a room to Jake Quincannon?"

"I don't see how you can ask that. Everyone in town knows what he is. He was a hood twenty years ago and you can tell just by looking at him that he's no better now. Just look at the way he dresses and that horrible eye patch. And that disgusting motorcycle."

She twisted her purse strap around her fingers, clearly agitated.

"God knows what he's been doing all these years, but you can bet it was something terrible. The man is obviously a menace. For all we know, he's escaped from some prison. He could be wanted by the law."

Paige half listened to Josie's babbling. She noticed that two of the town's most notorious gossips were studying a display of science books near the desk.

The front door opened and she glanced toward it, her eyes widening when she saw who was entering. Josie was oblivious of the sound of the door, oblivious of the ripple of shocked interest that swept through the library. She was only part way through her listing of Jake's faults.

"I don't know why he came back here in the first place. No one wants him here, everybody knows that. I think he came back just to see if he could cause trouble. And you have to go and help him by renting a room to him. Really, Paige, I don't see how you could be so stupid.

"It probably comes of having spent all that time reading. You don't understand the real world at all. But he's got to go. I'm sure Frank would be willing to ask him to leave, if you're afraid to do it yourself. I wouldn't blame you if you were. I don't know how you can stand looking at him with that awful thing over his eye."

Jake had come to a stop a little behind Josie, listening to the end of her speech without any expression on his face. Paige met his gaze. There was a certain bleak loneliness there that made her angry in a way all of Josie's foolish ramblings had failed to do.

"I don't need Frank to ask Jake anything, Josie," she said calmly. "Jake is welcome to stay as long as he likes. I've told him as much." She paused to give her furious sister a gentle smile before looking over Josie's shoulder. "Why, hello, Jake."

Time seemed to stop. Josie gasped, her eyes bulging unattractively as she realized that Jake had to have heard at least part of her tirade. Around them, the library was dead quiet. The sound of a pin falling would have reverberated like thunder.

Josie glared at Paige, a look Paige returned with a smile. As far as she was concerned, if Jake chose to tear Josie limb from limb, she'd earned it. Moving stiffly, Josie turned to face the man she'd so thoroughly vilified.

"I hadn't realized my past was quite so colorful, Josie." He sounded almost amused and Paige could see the color rise in her sister's cheek.

"I didn't realize you were there, Jake," she said stiffly.

"I've heard worse."

"I'm sure you have." It had taken Josie only a moment to regain her composure. Paige could see the gears turning. *After all, it wasn't as if she'd said anything that wasn't true. And she wouldn't have said anything at all if she hadn't been concerned about her baby sister.* Sometimes, Josie was so transparent, she was almost amusing.

"Obviously, I didn't intend for you to hear that, Jake, but perhaps it's just as well that you did."

"Well, I suppose it's better to know who your enemies are," Jake said, still with a touch of amusement in his voice.

Josie's fingers tightened over her purse. She didn't like the feeling that he was laughing at her. *No one* laughed at Josie Hudson.

"I'm not your enemy, Jake, but I *am* Paige's sister. Since our parents died, I'm the only family she has and it's only right that I should do my best to look out for her. After all, I am nearly eight years older than she is."

"Actually, it's thirteen years, Josie," Paige added helpfully. The look Josie threw her held little in the way of gratitude.

"Thirteen years," she said between clenched teeth. "You've been gone a long time, Jake," she continued, determined to make her point. "You may have forgotten what small towns are like."

"I've had plenty of reminders in the last few days," he said dryly.

"What I'm trying to say is that it may not have occurred to you that Paige could be harmed by your presence in her house. People do gossip. I'm sure you wouldn't want to damage her reputation."

"For heaven's sake, Josie, you sound like a dowager aunt in a regency novel," Paige said, irritated.

"You can laugh if you want to, Paige, but I'm sure Jake understands the seriousness of the situation."

Jake raised one eyebrow. "Are you expecting *me* to do the right thing and move out to protect her reputation? From what I heard when I came in, you seem to think I haven't a shred of moral fiber. What makes you think I'd give a damn about something like that?''

Caught in a trap of her own making, Josie was speechless.

''He's right, Josie. You can't have it both ways,'' said Mary, her expression thoughtful. The look Josie threw her should have withered her on the spot.

Paige looked past her furious sister to Jake.

''Were you just looking for a little abuse or did you come in for something specific, Jake?''

''You mean aside from giving the town something to gossip about?'' He glanced at the two matrons who'd gradually sidled closer to the scene of the action. Though there was nothing threatening in the look, they both flushed and set down the books they'd been holding. A moment later, the door closed behind them.

''Yes, aside from that,'' Paige said.

''Actually, I was heading out to Borden Hill. You'd said the library closed early today and I thought you might like to come along. But I hadn't realized that it might brand you a scarlet woman.''

''The library doesn't close for another two hours,'' Josie told him.

''I can take over for Paige.'' Mary's helpful offer earned her another of Josie's angry looks.

''You're not approved by the library committee.''

''She's approved by me,'' Paige said calmly. ''I'm sure they'll be delighted to have someone with a degree. I'd love to go with you, Jake.''

She opened the bottom drawer of the desk and took out her purse. ''You know where the keys are, Mary.''

"Don't worry about a thing." Mary rolled her eyes expressively in Jake's direction. "Have fun."

Paige knew Mary would grill her for every detail of the afternoon. Seeing Jake in the flesh had restored all of Mary's faith. Paige could call him "nice" if she wanted to, but Mary knew "dangerous" when she saw it. And she couldn't have been happier for her friend. In her opinion, a little danger was just what Paige needed in her life.

Chapter Six

Jake had begun to doubt the wisdom of asking Paige to go with him even before he got to the library. He'd only headed that way on an impulse, an impulse he'd half regretted even as he was pushing open the door. If it hadn't been for Josie, he might have made some vague excuse about wanting something to read and left it at that.

But as soon as he'd walked in on Josie's tirade, that option had disappeared. Thinking about the scene in the library, he acknowledged the foolishness of letting his anger get the best of him.

Paige's arms tightened around his waist as he leaned the bike into a curve. Hadn't he already decided that he'd keep his distance from Paige Cudahy? This was a fine way to keep that resolution.

He turned onto the dirt road that lead up the hill. Borden Hill had known various incarnations. There were caves on the north side, all but hidden by shrubbery, that were reputed to have provided hideouts for assorted bad guys in the 1880s.

Twenty-five years ago the hill had provided a place to park and neck. And the long road that wound up to the top had been the site of illicit drag races. Jake had participated in more than one of those until Pop Bellows, then Sheriff Bellows, had put a stop to the races by installing heavy iron gates at two critical points. The gates could be opened, of course, but there was only room for one car at a time to go through.

Jake bypassed the gates, steering the big bike around them, aware of Paige's arms tightening as they came near the edge of the road. In fact, he'd had a hard time concentrating on anything beyond the feel of her slim body pressed against his back.

This definitely was not in line with his policy of keeping distance between them.

Paige's hands slipped from his waist as he stopped the Harley and nudged the kickstand into place. He slipped off the bike, then offered Paige a hand. The skirt she was wearing today was neither as short nor as slim as the ones he'd seen her in before. He was grateful for that. As it was, that slender length of tanned leg was enough to put thoughts into his head that he didn't want to entertain.

"That was wonderful." She smiled up at him, running her fingers through her hair. It lay in wild tangles about her shoulders.

"I didn't think about your hair."

"Neither did I," she admitted. "I probably look like I'm wearing a haystack."

"There is a certain resemblance."

"Thanks. You're great for my ego." She threw him a reproachful look as she pulled a comb out of her purse.

Jake turned away as she began to work the tangles out. The view was just as he remembered it. The whole valley lay spread out before them. Riverbend lay in the distance, the river that had given the town its name curving protectively around its western edge. The air was warm and so still it was possible to hear the church bells in town ring the hour.

"It's beautiful up here," Paige said quietly. "I haven't been up here in years. I'd forgotten how pretty it was."

"This was one of my favorite places when I was a kid. From up here, anything seemed possible."

"Did you really plan on asking me up here or did you do it just to spite Josie?"

He glanced at her, wondering how he should answer the question. But she wasn't the kind of woman you lied to, not even if you'd been telling lies most of your life.

"A little of both," he admitted.

She chuckled, a deep rich sound that made him smile. "Josie never seems to understand that her attitude sometimes drives people to do the very thing she doesn't want them to do. It's one of the things that makes her tolerable. So, if Josie hadn't been carrying on, would you have asked me to go with you?"

She had the most disconcerting habit of asking irreverent questions. And the very fact that she asked them made it difficult to tell anything less than the truth.

"I don't know. I was planning on it and then it seemed like a foolish idea." He shrugged.

"I think it was a great idea. Actually, you more or less owed me this." He glanced at her, raising one eyebrow questioningly. "I've spent the whole day answering questions about you. The least you could do was offer me an escape."

"What did you tell them?"

"The truth, of course. I told them that you perform arcane rituals in the attic and that you're planning on resurrecting great bikers of the past to form The Motorcycle Gang From Hell to take over the town."

She said it with such relish that, for one startled moment, Jake wondered if she'd actually told people just that. His bewilderment must have shown in his face because she laughed.

"Only kidding. I was suitably vague. Really, from my description of you, everyone went away with the idea that you're the dullest thing in town. Let's sit over there. I like that tree."

She linked her arm through his unself-consciously, tugging him in the direction she wanted to go.

Paige settled herself on the scrubby grass beneath the tree, stretching her legs straight out in front of her as she leaned back on her elbows. Jake sat a little behind her, his back against the tree, one knee drawn up to serve as a prop for his elbow.

The silence that settled between them was nothing like the strained quiet that he felt when he was with his parents. It wasn't the same stillness he'd often felt when he was alone, preparing for a job. That had been a waiting kind of silence and there'd been a certain loneliness in it. But he'd grown so used to the loneliness that he rarely noticed it.

This was different. It wasn't a lonely silence and there was no strain in it, no feeling that she was waiting for him to say something or do something. Maybe this was what he'd been looking for when he'd thought of bringing her up here. There was a certain peace in her company, something he didn't find when he was alone.

"I'm sorry you heard Josie say the things she did." She spoke abruptly. From where he sat, Jake could see her in profile. She was frowning.

"Like I said, I've heard worse."

"She still shouldn't have said them. It's one thing to criticize the things you can do something about. I mean, if you really had no moral fiber, for example, then it wouldn't be so bad that she said so. Rude, of course, but honest. But she shouldn't have been so nasty about your eye."

Jake blinked, absorbing this novel way of looking at things. "So you're not sorry I heard her call me a hoodlum and say that I'd just come back to make trouble. But you *are* sorry I heard her make nasty remarks about the patch?"

"That's not exactly what I meant." She rolled over onto her stomach. Leaning on her elbows, she propped her chin in her hands as she looked at him. "Do you mind talking about it?"

"Talking about what?" He'd lost the thread again, just when he thought he'd figured out how to follow her thought processes.

"Your eye. Does it still hurt?"

"No." Funny, that was the first time anyone had asked him if it hurt. He couldn't even remember the doctors asking him that. They'd been more inclined to tell him what he would and wouldn't feel.

"When did it happen?" There was curiosity in the question but there was also concern for him, for what he'd gone through.

"A little over a year ago. I hardly think about it anymore."

"What happened? Was it an accident?"

"Only on my part," he said dryly. "Although, I guess you could say it was an accident on the part of the guy who had the knife, too. He was aiming for my throat."

"He was trying to kill you?" Her eyes widened, shocked.

"That was the general idea."

"How awful." Her synopsis of the event startled a laugh from him.

"It wasn't a whole lot of fun."

"Was it part of your job?"

"My job?" He looked vague, sorting quickly through a number of well-rehearsed answers.

"Mary thinks you must have been a spy, because of all the foreign stamps on the postcards you've sent your parents."

"Are spies the only ones who send postcards with foreign stamps?"

"No, but they're the most interesting possibility. Mary would be terribly disappointed to find out that you were an accountant who happened to work for an international firm."

"I hate to disappoint her. I did some government work but I'd hardly call myself a spy. More of a...courier, I suppose."

"A courier." She thought that one over while she reached out to pluck a dandelion. "Mary will be satisfied with that," she decided finally. "Not quite as good as being an international agent but close. Why did you quit?"

"How do you know I wasn't fired?" Just when he'd neatly skirted one topic, she came up with another one he wasn't sure how to address.

"I think you quit. I think it's part of the reason you came home."

"That pretty well sums it up," he admitted, slightly shaken to find his motives were so transparent to her.

"I thought so." Satisfied with her analysis, she blew on the dandelion, smiling as puffy white seeds dispersed.

She plucked another dandelion and rolled onto her back, twisting the stem between her fingers.

"So tell me how you came to be the local bad boy. I'm too young to remember all the heinous crimes you committed."

"I'm not sure I really committed any heinous crimes," Jake protested, vaguely disturbed that she seemed to take the whole thing so lightly.

"Oh, come on, you must have committed one or two." She rolled over again, propping her chin on one hand, twirling the dandelion between the fingers of her other hand. She watched him with such bright-eyed interest that Jake felt a smile tug at the corner of his mouth, finally breaking out in a full-blown grin.

"Do you manage to manipulate everyone into telling you all the details of their private lives?"

She frowned, considering. "Most people. So what did you do to get such a reputation?"

"Not much really." Jake's smile faded. He plucked a stalk of grass, pleating it distractedly between his fingers. "I was more obnoxious than dangerous, really. I had a chip on my shoulder the size of Montana and I guess it made people nervous. Not that I didn't commit a few minor misdemeanors in my time. I was the local drag king until Pop Bellows put up those gates."

He grinned reminiscently. "I considered trying to tear them down but I figured he'd tear a strip off me if I did."

"Pop Bellows? The old guard at the bank?"

"He was sheriff then and maybe I would have been a lot more serious about a career as a criminal if he hadn't been around."

"Were you afraid of *him*?" She sat up, curling her legs under her. He could see that she was having a hard time picturing the old man who dozed in his chair near the bank door as someone who might inspire fear in anyone.

"I had a healthy fear of the law. But that wasn't why I stayed out of real trouble. When I was fifteen, he caught me trying to steal a car. Since I fancied myself as pretty tough and had no intention of going to reform school, I came at him with a tire iron. He was smaller than I was and much older than I was—he must have been nearly fifty. I wasn't trying to kill him. I figured I'd just knock him out and then steal the car and make my getaway."

"What happened then?" Paige leaned forward, her attention focused on his story.

"I took one swing at him and next thing I knew I was flat on my back on the pavement and he was sitting on my chest. He had his leg across my throat, not putting any real pressure on, just lying there.

"I started to cuss and he leaned on the leg a little. He waited until I stopped seeing stars and then he began to talk. He informed me that I was the poorest excuse for a criminal he'd ever seen and that he wouldn't shame the jail by hauling me in. He explained every mistake I'd made in attempting to steal the car and then told me that I was a little too old to be so stupid.''

''What did you do?''

''There wasn't much I could do. Every time I started to speak, he'd put just a little pressure on that leg and cut my wind off.''

''You must have been scared.''

''Scared?'' Jake laughed, shaking his head. ''I was terrified. The longer he talked, explaining what I'd done wrong when I came at him with the tire iron, the more I began to think he was a lunatic. And you never know what a lunatic is going to do. Then he let me up and told me to come at him again.''

''Did you?''

''Sure. He was blocking the only way out of the alley. He threw me on the ground again. By about the third time he threw me, I was getting really angry. I tried everything I could think of but he tossed me on my butt every time.

''When I was finally too tired to try again, he hauled me onto my feet and started showing me how he was able to throw me so easily.''

Jake stared at the blade of grass he held, remembering the incident. The light from the streetlamps hadn't reached very far into the alley. Sheriff Bellows had stood there, lecturing him as calmly as if he were in a classroom. Jake had at least four inches and thirty pounds on the older man but it hadn't helped. If anything, it just meant the sheriff hit harder. He'd been battered and bruised and was nearly shaking with exhaustion when Bellows started showing him some of the self-defense techniques he'd used.

In the twenty-four years since then, Jake had learned half a dozen different forms of martial art. He

could use them all with deadly accuracy. He could kill
a man in more ways than he cared to name and hardly
miss a breath. But none of the lessons he'd learned
over the years had impressed him the way the one he'd
learned from Joe Bellows had.

"So he didn't arrest you?"

Paige's prompting made him realize that he'd been
sitting there staring into space for quite some time. He
shook himself back into the present.

"No, he didn't arrest me. He informed me that I
was to come into the office every day after school. I
could take out the trash and do odd jobs. In return,
he'd teach me what he could about self-defense."

"I'd almost forgotten that he was a sheriff," Paige
said, shaking her head. "Martin has held the job for
quite a while."

"Pop was damn good at his job. He knew how to
tell the difference between a criminal and a kid who
was just stupid enough to be looking for negative attention. If he'd arrested me, and he had every right to,
I'd probably have ended up a career criminal."

"Why didn't he arrest you? I mean, you didn't
really know him or anything, did you?"

"I asked him the same thing once and he just said
there was no sense in cluttering up the jails with people who were more stupid than they were dangerous."

She was quiet for a moment and then she sighed.
"That's an interesting story, Jake. It shows that you
can see someone all your life and never really notice
them that much. I'd never have pictured that old man
doing something like that. You were lucky."

"I think I was bright enough, even then, to figure
that out."

Paige shifted to sit beside him, settling her back against the tree trunk, stretching her legs out next to his. Her shoulder brushed against his. She was so close, he could catch the faint clean scent of her hair.

It seemed natural when his arm slipped around her shoulders, natural when she moved a little closer, settling comfortably into the curve of his arm. They sat in that position without speaking, looking out at the view.

It was as if the visit with his parents had happened a long time ago, and it seemed to have lost the importance it had at the time. Paige made no demands, offered no criticisms. She didn't watch him as if she expected him to explode at any moment. She didn't seem to think it incredible that he'd come home.

After she'd combed out her hair, she'd twisted it into a loose braid. The braid now fell against his chest, a pale streak across his black T-shirt. His hand came up and his fingers threaded through the braid, loosening it until her hair spilled over his hand like threads of sunlight.

"I'll have to braid it again," she murmured.

She tilted her head back to look at him and Jake's gaze shifted from her hair to meet her eyes. He could only guess what she saw in his face but he knew what he saw in hers. She looked curious and just a little bit wary. There was nothing concealed behind her eyes, no secrets lurking behind a plastic smile. In the shade cast by the tree's spreading branches, her eyes were dark green. Everything she felt, everything she thought was there for him to read.

Jake's hand cupped the back of her neck, his fingers slipping through her hair to cradle her head. Her eyes widened but she didn't protest as his head lowered toward hers.

Paige closed her eyes at the first touch of his mouth against hers. The soft brush of his mustache against her upper lip sent a shivery sensation down her spine. His lips were warm and firm. It was a slow, gentle kiss but there was a promise of heat behind it. She was drawn to that heat, at the same time knowing it could scorch as surely as it could warm.

Her hand came up to touch his cheek, feeling the faint scratchiness of a day's beard, the solid strength of his jaw. The kiss deepened, slowly, inevitably. It was as if all her life had been leading up to this one moment, here on a hilltop, with the rest of the world miles away.

Her lips parted beneath his but Jake didn't rush to accept the invitation she was extending. His tongue caressed her lower lip, trailed along the edge of her teeth before at last slipping inside to parry with hers.

Paige had been kissed before. She'd found it a pleasurable if slightly overrated experience. This kiss was nothing like any she'd ever known. She felt this kiss to the soles of her feet.

Need shot through her, catching her off guard, stripping away any defenses she may have had, leaving her open and vulnerable. Her fingers slid into the thick blackness of his hair as her breath left her on something perilously close to a sob.

Jake's hand tightened in her hair and then he shifted her, laying her back in the long grass without lifting his mouth from hers. Paige's arms came up to circle his shoulders, holding him against her as his mouth twisted over hers.

Neither of them had been prepared for the sudden rush of passion that exploded with the kiss. They'd been skirting their awareness of each other from the beginning, toying at the edges of it without really acknowledging it. Jake had been determined to keep his distance. Paige had no such clear-cut plan but she'd had no intention of getting involved in a relationship that was doomed to die even as the seasons changed.

With one kiss, everything had suddenly changed.

Jake lay half over her, supporting his weight on one elbow. His mouth assailed hers, demanding and receiving a response Paige hadn't realized she could give. Her fingers burrowed into his hair, wanting to draw him still closer.

His hand slid upward from her waist, resting against the side of her breast for a moment before moving to cup the full weight of her through her clothing. Paige shuddered, wrenching her mouth from his as his thumb brushed over her nipple. She stared up at him, her eyes wide, her mouth swollen.

His hand was still. His gaze was steady, holding something she couldn't read. For a moment, it seemed as if neither of them so much as took a breath. He didn't speak, didn't try to persuade her. Why was it so hard to say what she knew to be true?

"I don't think this is a good idea," she said slowly, her voice sounding strange to her ears. "I'm not ready for this."

The song of a meadowlark somewhere in the distance was the only sound to break the stillness. His hand shifted to the ground beside her and Paige's fingers slipped from his hair as he levered himself up and away.

A surprising sense of loss swept over her, so strong that for a moment she couldn't move. She shut her eyes, reminding herself that she'd done the right thing.

So why didn't it feel better?

THEY RODE HOME without speaking. Jake stopped at the house just long enough to let Paige off. Then he mumbled something about seeing her later and roared off into the gathering dusk.

Paige walked slowly up the pathway, aware that, across the street, Mrs. McCardle's curtain was open just far enough to allow one sharp eye to peer out. By tomorrow morning, it would be all over town that she'd gone riding on Jake Quincannon's big black Harley.

Letting herself into the house, she resisted the urge to turn and wave to the old busybody. She grinned at the image of Mrs. McCardle's shocked reaction to such a breach of etiquette. She'd lived in this town all her life and she could chart the path gossip took as clearly as if it were mapped out. Mrs. McCardle would call Essie Williams, who'd call Dodie Smith. From there, it would soon be common knowledge.

She kicked off her shoes in the hallway and headed for the kitchen, wondering, without much concern, just how garbled Mrs. McCardle's account would have become by tomorrow. At the very least, everyone would know that she'd had a passionate tryst with Jake. At worst, she would be pregnant with his child. Which would be quite a feat considering he'd been here less than a week. Still, little details like that had never bothered the grapevine before.

She pulled a carrot out of the crisper and rinsed it off before biting into it. Wandering over to the window, she stared out into the backyard, crunching absently. It was almost dark. Where had Jake gone?

She didn't doubt that he'd been upset by what had happened—or had almost happened—between them. He didn't want to get involved with her. She didn't need to be a mind reader to figure that one out.

She wasn't sure she wanted to get involved with him, either. She had other plans for her life, plans that didn't include a man with so many scars. It wasn't the physical scars that bothered her. It was the emotional ones; those would be hardest to heal.

If she had any sense at all, she'd ask him to move out. After all, he'd made it clear that he was only here for the summer. And involvement between them could last only as long as the lazy days of summer lasted. It was inevitable that she'd get hurt.

But for a little while, she'd be intensely alive.

She'd walked such a safe path all her life. What would it be like to throw caution completely to the wind? Jake was the most exciting thing to come into her life. But maybe the risk was too high. It was one thing to take a chance, it was something else again to commit emotional suicide.

Of course, there was always the question of whether *Jake* was interested in taking a chance.

IF THERE WAS ONE THING Jake knew, it was that he was not interested in taking chances. He'd spent his whole life doing that and he was tired of it. He'd left that life behind. He'd made his plans when he'd quit his job. He was going to do a little traveling, see all the places he'd only passed through. Then, in a year or two, he was going to buy a small piece of property, somewhere at a pleasant distance from the rest of the world, and he was going to sit and vegetate until moss grew on his north side.

Nowhere in those plans was there room for Paige Cudahy, not even as a summer affair. He'd come back here to bring completion to a part of his life that had been left unfinished. It hadn't been his intention to meet a long-legged woman with hair the color of sunshine. A woman without a self-conscious bone in her body. A woman nearly fifteen years younger than he was.

A woman who made him feel almost whole again.

He bent to pick up a stone, hurling it into the river with a violent movement that eloquently expressed his frustration. Paige had no place in his plans. It would be one thing if she were the kind of woman he could have a casual affair with, if he could then walk away without looking back. But Paige was the kind of woman who made a man want to look back.

Even if she were in his plans, he sure as hell wasn't in hers. He had too many scars, too many nightmares and too little to offer. He hardly knew who he was himself.

No, the best thing to do was to stick to the original plan and keep things between them casual. No more kisses like the one they'd shared today. That had been a mistake.

A mistake he certainly wouldn't repeat.

He threw another stone into the river, hearing the splash as it hit, though it was too dark to make out more than just the faint gleam of the moving water.

Hunching his shoulders against the chill that had entered the air as the sun went down, he wondered, yet again, if it hadn't been a mistake to come back here.

He could pack his bags and be gone in an hour. No one would be surprised. No one would miss him.

Except, maybe, Paige.

Staring at the dark water beneath him, he knew he wouldn't be leaving, at least not tonight.

Chapter Seven

"Jake!"

Jake turned at the sound of his name, narrowing his eyes against the sun that beat down on the concrete sidewalk. A girl waved at him from across the street, giving a perfunctory look right and left before darting across. It wasn't until she'd almost reached him that he realized who she was. Josie's daughter, Beth.

When he'd met her in Paige's kitchen, she'd been more casually dressed. Today she was wearing a crisp blue linen dress that complemented her eyes and dark hair.

"Should I call you Mr. Quincannon?" she asked, slightly breathless from hurrying. Just like her aunt, she didn't seem to feel any need to go through the usual formalities of polite conversation.

"Jake is fine."

"Good. Mr. Quincannon sounds old and fuddy-duddy and you don't look either one. Susie Rightman says you look like a pirate but I think that's much too obvious a comparison. I think you look more like a thwarted swain."

"A thwarted swain?" Despite himself, Jake grinned.

"Or a highwayman," she said, tilting her head to one side to look at him.

"You know, Paige was right, you don't even try to be tactful, do you?"

"I haven't found that being tactful is terribly useful," she told him solemnly. "Besides, I might as well get away with as much as I can while I'm young enough for people to think I'm cute."

Jake laughed. Beth Hudson had probably had everything she'd ever wanted and she was, he'd guess, a trifle spoiled. But there was a natural charm about her that suggested she didn't take herself too seriously and didn't expect anyone else to, either.

"I work at the bank. If you're heading that way, we could walk together."

"I've no objection." Jake turned, slowing his pace to suit her shorter stride. "I wanted to say hello to Pop, anyway."

"Good." She glanced up at him, her blue eyes sparkling with mischief. "Susie will be green with jealousy when she finds out I was seen with you."

"I gather Susie isn't one of your favorite people."

"She's a nasty little cat," Beth said, though there was no rancor in her tone. He had the feeling Beth didn't waste much time on disliking people.

"Would it help if I swept you up in my arms and carried you to the bank?" he asked.

"Would you really?" She looked up at him, her eyes wide and startled for a moment before she caught sight of the tuck in his cheek.

She laughed. "I don't think it's necessary to go quite that far. But thanks for the offer."

"It's the least I could do. No one's ever said I looked like a thwarted swain before."

He reached over her head to push open the door of the bank. Beth grinned up at him. "Anytime." She lifted her hand in farewell and moved off toward the rear of the bank, her quick steps holding a hint of bounce.

"Nice girl." Jake turned at Pop's comment, still half smiling. The old man was looking after Beth, a faint frown drawing his gray eyebrows together.

"She seems like a good kid. I thought I'd drop by to see if you were free to go for a beer, maybe some lunch."

"Sorry, Jake. I just got back from my lunch hour and Nathan would have a stroke if I took extra time. I swear, that man remembers every parking ticket I ever gave him."

Pop stood up, straightening with an effort. Jake glanced away, pretending not to notice how difficult the simple movement was for the older man. It hurt to see how old Pop had become. Twenty years ago, it had seemed as if nothing could ever age him. Stupid really. Time was the one thing no one escaped.

"Why don't you quit?" Jake asked.

"And do what? Sit home and wait to die?" Pop shook his head. "The problem is, I spent too much time on the job, Jake. I never married, never had kids. It was okay when I was younger. But once you get too old for the job, you don't have much left."

Listening to him, Jake felt a shiver run up his spine. He could see himself in the same place thirty or forty years from now. No one to care about, nothing but a job he couldn't do anymore. It was part of the reason he'd quit, but he'd had it in the back of his mind that he could always go back.

"You've made a lot of friends over the years, Pop. A lot of people admire you." Even as he said the words, he knew they offered cold comfort.

"Sure they do," Pop said easily. He smiled at Jake, his eyes faded but shrewd. "But it ain't enough. Don't ever get old, Jake, not alone, anyway. And don't let anyone tell you about the 'golden years.' Ain't nothing golden about them. Your reflexes slow, your bones ache when it's cold and sometimes they ache when it ain't cold."

There was no bitterness in the words, more a rueful acceptance of what couldn't be changed. But Jake could hear the loneliness beneath the touch of humor.

He talked with Pop for a few more minutes until he noticed Henry Nathan hovering in the doorway of his office, a scowl on his overfed face. Not wanting to give the bank president a reason to harass Pop, Jake made his farewells and left the bank.

Standing on the sidewalk, he shoved his hands into the back pockets of his jeans. The sun was hot on his back. There was no place he had to be, no one was expecting him to go anywhere or do anything. He could go see his parents, but his last visit had been neither pleasant nor productive.

"You know, we have laws about loitering."

Jake turned to face Martin Smith, raising his eyebrows. "You going to arrest me, officer?"

"Not today. It's too hot for arresting people. In order to get you off the streets, though, I'll buy you a beer."

A few minutes later they were seated across from each other at Pat's Place, a combination beer bar and café. The cracked red vinyl booths were probably the

same ones Jake remembered. He'd earned the money
to buy his first bike cleaning the kitchen here.

"Pat Roberts still run this place?" he asked Martin
after the waitress brought their order—beer for Jake
and a soda for Martin, who was on duty.

"Pat died about eight years ago. His nephew moved
up here from Texas and took the place over. He put in
a new pool table, but other than that, nothing has
really changed."

"Sounds like the whole town," he commented,
reaching for the icy beer.

"Just like living in the fifties," Martin agreed.
"Change comes slow here."

"Doesn't seem like change comes here at all."

"Sure it does. Old man Dearborn just sold the '62
Buick he bought new. Bought himself a brand-new
pickup."

Catching the laughter in Martin's eyes, Jake shook
his head, smiling. "Like I said, nothing changes in this
town."

They talked easily. Martin might have made the
choice to come back to Riverbend, but he hadn't lost
sight of how the rest of the world had changed. Talking with him, Jake didn't feel as much like an alien
invader as he did when talking to most of the towns-
people.

Jake couldn't have said just how it was that the
subject got around to Paige. He certainly hadn't
planned on talking about her. In fact, he'd been doing
his best to avoid her since that disturbing kiss they'd
shared nearly two weeks ago. He hadn't even let his
thoughts settle on her for more than a moment or two.

It was inevitable that, living in the same house,
they'd run into each other from time to time, but he'd

made a point of not doing more than to exchange a polite greeting and then make his exit. It wasn't that he was running away. But a wise man knew his limits and he had a feeling that Paige could push him past limits he didn't even know he had.

Yet, somehow, her name had come up.

"Sure, Paige left home." Martin drained the last of his soda, gave Jake's beer a longing glance and signaled the waitress to bring them another cold drink. "I wasn't home then, but Mary filled me in on what happened. She and Paige are pretty close."

"Little brunette with bright eyes?" Jake remembered the woman who'd volunteered to cover for Paige at the library.

"That's Mary. We're planning on getting married next April."

He took a drink from the fresh glass of soda before going on. "Anyway, Paige went off to college, all the way to L.A. But she'd only been gone a couple of years when her father had a heart attack and died. Paige came home for the funeral, of course. Her mother was pretty shaken up and Josie wasn't a whole lot of help. So Paige stayed to help her mother get on her feet again. Only a couple of months after her father died, her mother had a stroke.

"Josie was all for putting her in a nursing home, but Paige said her mother wouldn't want that. She kept her at home and took care of her. Mrs. Cudahy lived three more years. She never got out of bed, never could talk."

"Paige could have gone back to school after her mother died," Jake said.

"She could have, but I think she'd lost the drive for it. By then, she'd taken the job at the library, though they had their doubts about hiring someone as young as she was. But there wasn't anyone else beating down the door for the job, so Paige got it. And then, her folks had left her the house. Josie was the apple of their eye but I think they knew she had no feelings for the place. She'd tear it down and put up a condo if she could."

An insistent noise interrupted him. Muttering a mild curse, Martin reached down to shut off his beeper.

"Duty calls. Someone probably lost the keys to the jail." He slid out of the booth. "I'll be seeing you around."

Jake lifted his hand in farewell, watching the sheriff leave before returning a brooding gaze to his nearly empty beer glass.

It was bad enough being attracted to Paige and trying to keep his distance. It only made it worse that the more he learned about her, the more he found himself liking her.

THE LIBRARY WAS CLOSED on Wednesdays, which was one of the reasons Jake had left the house early, before Paige was out of bed. But he found himself drifting back as the sun began to set over the western mountains. Having thought about little else all afternoon, he'd realized that avoiding Paige was an impractical solution to the problem.

They lived in the same house and there was a limit to the number of things he could find with which to occupy himself in a town the size of Riverbend. Besides, he'd come home to find a certain peace within himself and he couldn't do it if he was dodging his landlady like a five-year-old trying to avoid a bath.

Stepping through the front door, he drew in a deep, appreciative breath. The scent of garlic drifted from the kitchen, rich and inviting. Before he could decide whether or not to follow that invitation, Paige stuck her head out of the kitchen, looking at him with those wide green eyes that had haunted more of his dreams than he cared to admit.

"I thought I heard you come in. Are you going to be here for dinner?"

"Am I invited to have whatever you're cooking?"

"Of course. I only cook once or twice a year but I always cook enough for thirty or forty people."

"The way it smells I may be able to eat enough for thirty or forty people."

"Good. Why don't you go pick up Beth and a bottle of wine?"

Thirty minutes later, Jake pulled up in front of a big two-story house, more suited to the Deep South than Idaho. Massive white pillars marched across the front of the wide porch and he wouldn't have been surprised to see Scarlett O'Hara come sweeping down the steps onto the huge expanse of lawn.

Looking at it, he had no trouble attributing its wholly inappropriate design to Josie's pretensions. It was obviously designed to impress the peons in town, but Jake suspected it had elicited more laughter than anything else.

Swinging himself off the bike, he walked up the long brick path. His boots sounded loud on the wooden porch floor. The doorbell rang an elegant peal somewhere inside the big house. When the door swung open, he found himself face-to-face with Josie—the first time he'd seen her since the incident at the library.

She stared at him, her fair skin flushing and then paling.

"What are you doing here?"

"Paige asked me to pick up Beth."

"Beth?" Her voice rose on the name, her eyes flickering with some expression he couldn't read.

"Mom, is that Jake?" Beth's voice came down the stairs ahead of her. Josie's fingers tightened over the edge of the door, and for a moment, Jake had the feeling she was going to slam the door and tell her daughter it had been someone else there. If that was on her agenda, she must have thought better of it. Instead, she tried a different tack.

"Where do you think you're going? You have to work tomorrow."

Through the open door, Jake could see Beth coming down the stairs. She was wearing jeans and a loose shirt, her dark hair flying out behind her.

"I'm just going to Aunt Paige's for dinner. She's making scampi. She called to let me know Jake would be picking me up." She looked past her mother at Jake, who was still standing on the doorstep. "Did you bring your motorcycle?"

"I won't have you riding on that awful machine, Elizabeth."

"Mom, it's perfectly safe. Jake is very careful, aren't you, Jake?"

"I haven't had an accident yet," he said noncommittally.

"I don't see how you can possibly drive that thing, what with having one eye and all." Josie's gaze flicked over his face and then away, as if the sight of the patch disgusted her.

"Mother!" Beth was shocked by the blatant cruelty of her mother's remark. Josie flushed, but she set her chin stubbornly in a look Jake remembered thinking rather cute when they were dating.

"I'm sorry if I've hurt your feelings," she said, though making her apology sound to the contrary. "But Beth is my daughter and I have to look out for her safety."

"Mother, don't fuss so much. I'm nineteen, not nine. *I* trust Jake and that's what matters."

Jake stayed quiet. It wasn't his place to interfere even if Josie's objection had little or nothing to do with Beth's safety.

"What's the problem here?" Frank stepped out into the hallway, taking in the confrontation between his daughter and his wife in a moment. From the way he immediately stepped forward, Jake had the feeling that the scene was not a new one.

"Hello, Jake." Frank stopped behind Josie, putting his hands on her shoulders and smiling at Jake over her head. "That must have been you I heard ring the bell a few minutes ago. What are you doing still standing on the doorstep?"

Jake let his gaze linger on Josie's face until she flushed, her eyes angry as she waited for him to say that he hadn't been invited inside. He waited for the space of several slow heartbeats before lifting his gaze to Frank's.

"I just stopped by to pick up Beth. Paige asked me to bring her to dinner."

"Is Paige doing her annual cooking spree?" Frank grinned and Jake saw that his front teeth were slightly crooked, just as they had been when they were both boys. He half smiled.

"I gather she doesn't do this very often."

"Once or twice a year. Well, Beth, you'd better hurry before the food gets cold."

"Frank, I already told Beth I didn't want her riding on that motorcycle."

"And I already told Mother I was old enough to make my own decisions."

"Don't speak to your mother in that tone, Beth," Frank told her gently, but with a note in his voice that made her flush and mumble an apology.

"I'm sure she'll be fine, Josie."

"But—"

His hands tightened on her shoulders and she broke off, her eyes dropping to the floor. "Jake will take care of her, won't you, Jake?"

"I haven't lost a passenger yet."

Beth slipped out the door before anyone could change their minds. Jake nodded to Frank, glanced at Josie's still lowered face and turned to follow Beth, who was already halfway down the path.

THE DINNER WAS A SUCCESS. Paige might not bother to cook very often but it was clear that it wasn't because she lacked culinary talent. The shrimp were juicy and moist, redolent of garlic and butter, the rice pilaf was delicately seasoned, the vegetables perfectly cooked. And to top off the meal, she'd made an enormous apple pie, laced with heavy cream poured in just before it finished baking.

She hadn't cooked enough for forty people but she'd cooked more than enough for the small gathering she'd invited. Aside from herself, Jake and Beth, Martin and Mary were the only other guests.

It had been a long time since Jake had been part of a dinner party of any sort. Small talk was a skill he'd lost a long time ago, and as soon as he'd accepted Paige's invitation, he'd doubted the wisdom of it. He needn't have been concerned. These were people who'd known each other a long time and they included him in their small circle as if he'd been there all along.

The talk ranged from the latest news from Europe to whether or not Ethel Levine's hair actually grew out pale blue or whether she had it dyed in the dead of night since no one had ever seen her enter a hair salon.

After the meal, they moved into the living room. Jake deliberately chose a seat that fell just beyond the circle of light cast by the lamps. It was a habit, always sticking to the shadows.

He watched as Beth ran and got Paige's guitar from her bedroom, pushing it into her aunt's hands. Laughing, Paige strummed a few chords and then broke into a chorus of "Bottle of Wine."

Everyone joined in, just as she'd intended them to. Watching the others, Jake wondered what it must be like to feel so completely comfortable in the company of other people, to be able to relax and not fear revealing something you didn't want them to know.

An hour later, the more boisterous songs had given way to soft folk ballads. Martin had his arm around Mary's waist, her head resting on his shoulder. Beth sat on the floor, leaning back against the sofa.

Paige's voice was not particularly beautiful, but there was something about the husky contralto that wrapped itself around the music. Accompanied by vaguely minor chords, she sang of loves lost and found, of destinies intertwined. Jake thought it might be possible to lose himself in that voice.

She'd just finished a song about a gypsy's lost love, the last chord still quivering in the air, when the mantel clock chimed the hour. Jake counted the bells, surprised when they reached eleven.

"You'd better get home, Beth, before your mother sends out a search party." Ignoring Beth's automatic protest, Paige set down the guitar.

"And I've got to go to work tomorrow," Martin said. He stood up, drawing Mary to her feet. "We can give you a ride, Beth. Saves Jake having to make a special trip."

Jake lingered in the living room as Paige saw her guests to the door. He was trying to convince himself of the wisdom of going upstairs, when Paige came back.

"There's most of a bottle of wine left," she said by way of greeting. "It seems a shame to let it go to waste."

Jake took the bottle from her and filled both their glasses.

"I'm glad you decided to stay," she said a few minutes later. She was sprawled in a big leather chair, her legs draped comfortably, if inelegantly, across the arm.

"So am I. You have nice friends."

"It's the only kind to have. Where did you find this wine? It's nothing like the stuff they carry at Burt's Market."

"The new liquor store on the edge of town has a pretty decent selection." Jake swirled the Chardonnay in the glass before taking a sip. "Nothing fancy, but some decent stuff."

"Are you implying that the wine at Burt's Market isn't first-rate? I'll have you know some of that stuff has been aged for more than a month in aluminum tanks. Some of them even had an oak log or two floating in them. But you have to watch out for the splinters with those."

"I'm sure Burt has a lovely selection of varietals," Jake said solemnly.

"You'd better watch what you say about Burt. I'm sure he'd never allow a varietal in the place." She raised her nose in the air, looking very haughty. "He does have his standards, you know."

Jake grinned. "I'm sure he does. I wouldn't dream of casting aspersions on Burt's standards."

"I think it's illegal to cast aspersions in Riverbend."

"Probably."

A comfortable silence fell between them, broken only by the ticking of the clock on the mantel. Somewhere in the distance, a dog barked a few times and then was quiet.

"What's it like to travel all over the world?"

Jake shifted his gaze from his glass to her. She'd shut off most of the lamps when the others left, leaving one to hold back the darkness. Jake could see only her profile and the pale length of her hair. She looked, he thought, rather wistful.

"It's not as exciting as it seems," he answered at last. "After a few years one place looks much like another."

"Have you been to Paris?"

"A couple of times."

"What's it like? Is it as romantic as they say?"

"It's pretty, I guess." Jake struggled to remember what Paris had been like—not the Paris he'd known, which had been dark alleys and information passed surreptitiously in the night. That wasn't the Paris she was talking about. She wanted to know about Paris in the springtime; lovers walking along the Champs-Elysées; rich coffee in quaint little cafés.

"And Rome? Have you ever been there? Or Athens? Is the Acropolis as beautiful as it looks in pictures?"

Jake tried to answer her questions about the places he'd been, groping for images of things only half seen. How could he tell her that he was more familiar with the back alleys of the world's great cities than with their museums? He could have instantly named half a dozen hidden corners of London where a rendezvous would go unnoticed, but Buckingham Palace was only a dim memory.

The clock rang once as Paige poured the last of the wine, dividing it evenly between her glass and Jake's.

"You've seen so much of the world," she said, setting the empty bottle on the hearth before sinking back into her chair.

"A good part of it, I guess." Jake wondered if she knew that those wispy little bangs gave her a pensive look.

"I went to L.A. once. I was going to get my degree and then find some job where I could travel. I was going to go all over the world." She gestured expansively, the wine sloshing dangerously close to the edge of her glass. "But then, my father died and my mother fell ill. So I came back here to look after her."

"You could have hired someone to take care of her."

"I suppose." She sighed, cradling the glass between her palms, staring at the pale liquid as if she were seeing pictures in it. "But Mom wouldn't have liked that, having a stranger take care of her. She was a very private person.

"We weren't close, you know." She turned her head to look at him, so much vulnerability in her eyes that Jake wanted to take her in his arms and hold her, keep her safe.

"But you took care of her, anyway."

"Yeah." She sighed again, leaning her head back against the chair, closing her eyes. "People in town thought that I was very noble and self-sacrificing but I really did it for selfish reasons."

"You quit school and came home to nurse your mother for selfish reasons?"

She didn't open her eyes but she must have heard the disbelief in his tone. She half smiled. "I really did."

"How was it selfish?"

"We never seemed to connect when I was little. It wasn't that she and Dad didn't love me. I always knew they loved me but they didn't quite know what to do with me. I was a surprise baby. After Josie, they never expected to have another child, so they gave everything they had to give to her. When I came along, it was hard for them to shift gears and include me in the family. And I was so bookish. I think they thought it was unnatural to always be reading."

There was no rancor in her tone, no recollected hurt. But Jake knew the hurt was there. He knew what it was like to be an outcast in your own family, to never quite fit in no matter how hard you tried. Pretty soon you gave up trying, but you never got over wondering what you'd done wrong.

"Anyway, when Mom had her stroke, the doctor told us that it was unlikely she'd ever fully recover. She was going to have to have full-time care. So I decided to take care of her myself. I thought maybe, if we had the chance, we could find some common ground."

"And did you?"

"I think so. She couldn't talk but we found ways to communicate. She could blink and she could move her fingers a little. It sounds funny but I think we really got to know each other in those last couple of years."

She finished the last of her wine, settling deeper still into the big chair. "It was worth giving up college for that. I always thought I'd leave after she died, but somehow, I just never got around to it." The words trailed off on a yawn.

Without meaning to, Paige had summed up exactly what he was looking for—a common ground. Not just with his family but with the world in general.

He'd spent so many years living on the outside. At first by choice and then because he didn't know how else to live. The time he'd spent recovering from the fight that had cost him his eye had given him a chance to think about his life—where it had been, where it was going. In an odd way, it was as if losing his eye had made him really see.

He shook his head. Maybe he'd had too much wine. This unaccustomed bout of philosophizing was hardly his style. But then he'd been doing a lot of uncharacteristic things lately. Like spending time thinking about a woman he had no intention of getting involved with.

Glancing at Paige, he felt the illogical twinge of resentment fade. While he'd been pondering the meaning of his life—or the lack thereof—she'd fallen asleep. She looked so vulnerable. It wasn't just himself he was trying to protect. He didn't want to hurt her.

Jake set his glass down and got up. She sighed when he removed her empty wineglass and placed it on the hearth. He lifted a hand that had been dangling over the floor and laid it across her body, but she didn't awaken. She slept like a child, her lips slightly parted, her face as innocent as a babe's.

The only practical thing to do was to wake her up and send her off to bed. But she looked so peaceful, so completely relaxed.

She weighed next to nothing in his arms. She stirred as he lifted her, but only to settle closer, to press her cheek to his shoulder. Jake carried her upstairs and into her bedroom, angling her feet through the doorway.

It was the first time he'd been in her room. In the darkness he could make out little beyond the vague shapes of bed and dresser. She sighed as he laid her on the bed, turning her face into the pillow. His hands left her reluctantly as he straightened.

Without thinking, he reached out to brush a lock of hair from her cheek. It slipped through his fingers like fine silk. He wanted to sink his fingers in her hair. He wanted to feel her awaken under his touch, feel her melt under his mouth.

With an effort, he stepped away from the bed. Maybe he really *had* had a little too much wine. Or maybe his willpower just wasn't what it had been.

He'd almost reached the door when her voice caught him.

"Good night, Jake. I'm glad you stayed tonight." Her voice was slurred with sleepiness, and glancing back over his shoulder, Jake saw that she'd turned on her side, her hands tucked under cheek, apparently more than half asleep.

She looked like his destruction.

She looked like heaven on earth.

It took all his diminishing willpower to continue walking out the door.

Chapter Eight

The annual Fourth of July picnic was one of the great events on Riverbend's calender. Cynics might have said it was the *only* great event. But even the cynics had to admit that the weekend was a genuine, small-town extravaganza.

A traveling carnival rolled into town the week before the holiday, setting up a haunted house, a Ferris wheel, a merry-go-round and enough rides to please even the most demanding youngsters. There were also shooting galleries and various games that enabled young men to show off their dubious skills as they attempted to win neon-pink stuffed animals for their dates.

People poured into town from miles away and Riverbend took on an atmosphere of unaccustomed bustle. There were horse races and shooting contests where the locals vied for prizes ranging from gift certificates for Hank's Feed and Seed to a new calf.

It was, Paige thought, her favorite holiday of the year. Especially this year. Dipping her hand into the bag of caramel corn that was sure to ruin her appetite for dinner, she glanced sideways at Jake. As usual, his expression was difficult to read. He didn't seem to work consciously on keeping his thoughts hidden. He didn't have to. It was, she suspected, a habit ingrained over the years. It would be interesting to know just what he'd done for a living since getting out of the service. She didn't, for a minute, believe that he'd been a courier—or at least not *only* a courier.

One thing he hadn't been was a ladies' man, she thought with a grin. The extreme, offhand way he'd asked her if she'd like to go to the fair with him was hardly the sort of thing to make a girl's heart go pitter-patter.

She grinned. From the expression he'd worn, she hadn't been able to tell whether he was glad or sorry that she'd accepted. He'd stopped avoiding her since the night he'd carried her up to bed. In fact, they'd eaten together more nights than not since then. She wasn't surprised by the fact that Jake was a more than passable cook. She had the feeling that he was probably pretty good at anything he set his mind to.

But even though he wasn't going out of his way to avoid her, there was a reserve in his attitude toward her. A reserve at odds with the way he sometimes looked at her. She hadn't quite made up her own mind about where this relationship was headed, or where she *hoped* it was headed. But wherever it was going, she was willing to go along with it. At least for now.

"What are you smiling about?"

She glanced up, meeting his gaze. "I was just remembering how shocked you looked to find yourself asking me for a date."

"I wasn't shocked. Besides, this isn't a date," he protested with an uneasiness that made her grin widen.

"Sure it is." She reached for another handful of caramel corn. "When a man asks a woman to go somewhere with him, it's a date," she informed him with precise logic.

"Dating is something teenagers do."

"You don't have to be sixteen to go on a date. If you didn't want to go out with me, you shouldn't have asked me."

"The trouble with you is that you didn't get enough spankings when you were little," he told her. "You have no respect for your elders."

"My elders?" She raised her eyebrows in a gesture of exaggerated disbelief. She stopped as if struck, turning to look at him. There was a deep tuck in his cheek that told her he was holding back a smile. It was an expression she'd become familiar with over the last month and she found the urge to coax that smile out of hiding more and more irresistible.

"You know, now that you mention it, I suppose you are just about over the hill. Maybe we should buy you a cane. And you forgot to ask for the senior citizen's discount at the gate."

"Brat." He reached out, taking hold of her thick braid and tugging on it. "Like I said, someone should have spanked you regularly."

She tilted her head to one side, her spirit not visibly dampened. "You should smile more often, Jake. Did you know you have a dimple right there?"

She reached up to touch his cheek, setting her finger in the shallow indentation there. The small contact sent a warm tingling sensation up her arm. Her gaze lifted to his and the tingle spread down her back. She felt his hand tighten on her braid, drawing her closer.

Was he going to kiss her right here in the middle of the fair, where half the town would be sure to know about it before sundown? Did she care if everybody knew that she and Jake Quincannon were on the verge of becoming something more than mere acquaintances?

Not particularly.

But as it happened, she didn't get a chance to prove it.

Just when a kiss seemed inevitable, Jake suddenly seemed to realize where they were. He drew back, releasing her braid, almost shaking himself as if trying to snap himself awake.

Paige drew in a breath, plunging her hand into the sack of caramel corn, trying to look as if nothing had happened. Which, of course, it hadn't.

"Jake! Hey, Jake!"

They both turned in answer to the summons. Jake's face broke into a grin. Pop waved to him from beneath a purple-and-yellow striped awning. Paige followed him over to the booth.

She'd known Pop Bellows all her life. But remembering the story Jake had told her, she found herself seeing him with new eyes. Looking at the two of them together, it was hard to imagine a time when Pop had been able to physically best Jake. It was funny how Time had a way of reversing people's positions in life.

"Paige Cudahy, what are you doing with this good-for-nothing?" As he glanced at Jake, Pop's eyes sparked with an affection that belied his words.

"I thought he might need someone to take care of him."

Pop chuckled. "You be sure to keep him out of trouble."

"I can keep myself out of trouble, Pop."

"Maybe. Maybe not. But if I had a girl as pretty as that willing to look after me, you can bet I'd try to find a bit of trouble just for the pleasure of letting her keep me out of it."

"I'll keep that in mind," Jake said, slanting an inscrutable look in Paige's direction.

"Aunt Paige!" Paige turned to see Beth hurrying toward them, a somewhat sullen-looking Billy Wilson in tow. "Isn't this fun? Hi, Jake."

Youthful enthusiasm bubbled in her voice, her blue eyes sparkling with pleasure.

"Hi, Beth. Billy." It took an effort for Paige to nod pleasantly to the narrow-faced youth standing behind Beth. How a girl as pretty and intelligent as her niece had settled on a scuzzy little weasel like that, was a question Paige couldn't answer.

"Did you just get here? You've got to ride on the Ferris wheel. It's higher than the one they had here last year." Beth paused to draw a breath and glanced into the booth they were standing in front of. "Oh, look at that adorable little kitty cat," she exclaimed, looking at a fluffy white stuffed cat on the top shelf.

Sensing he had a customer, the man behind the counter smiled at Beth, displaying a rather awe-inspiring number of teeth. "That's our highest prize, little lady. Why don't you give it a whirl? All you got to do is hit the little ducks with the rifle and you can take the stuffed animal home."

"Billy?" Beth turned to the youth, her voice coaxing.

"I already told you I ain't no good at these dumb games," he muttered, throwing a surly look at the man behind the counter. "I didn't want to come to this stupid carnival in the first place."

Paige's fingers itched with the urge to smack him. Beth's look of eagerness faded, squashed more by his boorishness than by the loss of the stuffed cat she probably wouldn't have ended up with anyway.

"If you really want the cat, I could give it a try." Jake's offer brought Paige's eyes to his face. From the glance he threw Billy, she guessed that he found the boy as unpleasant as she did.

"Would you really, Jake?" Beth's spirits rebounded, her face breaking into a wide smile. Then she glanced at Billy, obviously concerned about his reaction. "You wouldn't mind, would you?"

Billy looked as if he was about to say that he minded very much, but after a quick glance at Jake, he mumbled something about it being no skin off his nose. Paige bit her lip to hold back a smile. She'd caught only the edge of the look Jake had given the boy but she wasn't surprised Billy had changed his response.

"Now, we'll see some shooting," Pop said quietly as Jake picked up the rifle. Jake studied the duck silhouettes that paraded back and forth near the back of the tent and then lifted the toy gun to his shoulder. Six shots later, five of the metal silhouettes had disappeared.

"Oh, too bad. Nearly a perfect score." The man who ran the booth was eyeing Jake uneasily, disliking the easy way he handled the gun. "I'll tell you what, I'll give the little lady a consolation prize."

"No." Jake pulled a handful of change out of his pocket and set it on the counter. "She wants the stuffed cat." He picked up the rifle again.

"When he was a kid, Jake was the best shot I ever saw," Pop told Paige quietly. "I'd wondered if losing his eye would have affected that."

"It doesn't look like it has." Paige watched Jake lay out the little metal ducks.

"He was a good boy," Pop said suddenly. Paige glanced at the old man, surprised to see him looking at her so intently.

"Jake told me how you caught him trying to steal a car."

Pop smiled, his faded eyes alight with memories. "Worst car thief you ever saw. But he was a good kid. A bit of a hell-raiser and he never knew when to back down. People got the idea in their heads that he was trouble and he could never quite get out from under that reputation. That's the worst thing about a small town. Once they poke you in a slot, you stay there forever."

Jake annihilated another half a dozen ducks. The man behind the counter had given up looking uneasy. Now he just looked resigned. Beth squealed as each new round was demolished. Billy looked as if he'd just swallowed something with a nasty taste. As usual, there was little to be read in Jake's expression.

"He doesn't show much of himself, does he?" Paige asked.

"That's the way a lot of folks deal with bein' hurt," Pop said. "His folks had a real problem with him. After his brother died, it seemed as if Jake couldn't do anything right."

"His brother?" Paige's head jerked around, her eyes startled. "I didn't know Jake had a brother."

"No reason you should. You weren't even born when he died. Jake was only about six or seven. He don't talk about it. Neither do his folks. Fact of the matter is, I think most folks around here have forgotten there was another boy. But Jake hasn't forgotten.

He talked with me about it once. Only time I ever heard him mention it. It was that time he came home after he left to join the service."

When he'd come home to find Josie married to Frank.

"What happened to his brother, Pop?" Pop studied her for a long silent moment, as if trying to decide whether to tell her.

"Well, I don't know all the details. It was a long time ago. Jake, he'd been drinking real heavy or he wouldn't have told me at all, I reckon. The boy was two or three years younger than Jake, so I guess he'd have been about four when he died. Jake said he was the prettiest little thing you ever did see. He had blond hair and blue eyes, looked just like an angel. The apple of their mother's eye, too. I don't know exactly what happened to him. Leastaways, if Jake told me, I don't remember. Some sort of accident, I think."

Pop paused and ran a hand over his thinning hair. "I pieced a bit of this together myself, you understand. Near as I can figure, after his little brother died, there just wasn't nothin' Jake could do that his folks didn't find fault with. He seemed to think they blamed him for being alive when the little one was dead."

"That's awful. He was just a little boy himself."

"People do funny things when they're grieving. Maybe they didn't mean to push him away, maybe they were trying to protect themselves against loving him too much, lest something happen to him, too."

"That's no excuse. He was hardly more than a baby himself."

"I ain't making excuses for their behavior. I'm just offering ideas." Pop's eyes narrowed on her. "Maybe I shouldn't have told you any of this. It ain't really any of my business. But that boy's been hurt a good bit in his life. I don't know what all he's been up to since he left, but you can see in his face that it ain't been a bed of roses. I'd surely hate to see him get hurt again.''

It wasn't hard to understand what he was saying. He thought *she* might hurt Jake. She had the feeling that if anyone was going to get hurt, it wasn't going to be Jake. She bent and brushed a kiss over the old man's cheek.

''Jake is very lucky to have a friend like you.''

Beth's ecstatic squeal interrupted anything Pop might have said in response. Paige turned to see the stuffed cat being handed across the counter. Beth clutched it to her with one arm and threw the other around Jake's neck.

''Thank you, thank you, thank you.'' She planted a kiss on his cheek. For once, Paige had no difficulty reading his expression. The mixture of uneasy pleasure and embarrassment was easy to see and rather endearing.

She moved over to the little group, noting with amusement that Billy looked even more sour than he usually did.

''Now that the great white hunter has bagged his game, do you think we could go eat?'' He threw her a grateful look. It seemed perfectly natural to slip her arm through his as they moved off down the wide dirt fairway.

''You really made Beth's day,'' she commented.

''It was no big deal.''

''And you ruined Billy's,'' she said with relish.

''I can see why you don't like the guy. I hope I wasn't that sullen when I was his age.''

''You were more the brooding type.''

"Brooding? Makes me sound like a chicken."

"That's broody and it's something else entirely. Look, there's a corn dog stand."

"You can't really be hungry," Jake protested, as she led him across the fairway. "You just ate all that sweet stuff."

"And now I'm ready for some real food. Come on, don't they smell good?"

"Do you know what they put in a hot dog?"

"No and I don't want to know." She ordered two corn dogs, thrusting one of them into Jake's hand. "It's not a real Fourth of July unless you have a corn dog."

If the truth were known, Jake suspected he'd eat a stick if she gave it to him with that persuasive smile. He'd never been particularly crazy about the Fourth of July picnic when he was a kid. But seeing it through Paige's eyes, he was discovering new pleasures in it.

She had the ability to see things as a child would see them. She didn't see the garishness of the painted rides or the cheap costumes or the fact that, in the end, the house always won at any of the foolish games of skill. She enjoyed the spectacle of it, oohing and aahing over tricks that were as old as Methuselah, responding to them as if she hadn't seen them a hundred times before.

It was, he decided, not a bad way to look at life.

Halfway through the afternoon, they bumped into Martin and Mary. The four of them wandered through the fair. Martin won Mary a vaguely obscene-looking Kewpie doll at the ringtoss and Paige insisted on trying her hand at dunking the clown. Her throws were so wild, there was more danger of her giving him a concussion than of her hitting the target to dunk him.

Jake couldn't remember the last time he'd laughed so much.

It was late afternoon when they found themselves at the edge of the field that served as the fairgrounds. The rifle shooting contest was due to start in a few minutes and, from the size of the crowd, it was obvious that this was one of the major events of the fair.

More by accident than anything else, they found themselves near the front of the crowd. Jake looked over the setup and the contestants with professional interest. They were a mixed bunch; farmers, ranchers, some old, some young. Some of these men provided a good bit of the meat for their families by hunting. Some of them looked deadly serious, and some of them looked as if they were just having a good time.

"Are you going to enter, Jake?" He glanced around, startled by the suggestion. He hadn't noticed Beth's approach.

"I don't think so."

"Come on. You're really good. Tell him he should enter, Dad. I told you how he won my cat."

Jake's gaze went over her head to where Frank stood. "Hello, Jake. Beth tells me you're still pretty good with a rifle." Frank was carrying his rifle tucked under his arm, barrel down, a box of shells in his hand.

"I can hold my own," Jake said. How many times had they competed as boys? Taking potshots at cans and bottles, they'd been evenly matched then.

"Are you going to enter, Jake?" Beth asked again.

"I don't think so." He shook his head. "I don't even have a gun."

"I've got one in the car," Martin offered.

"Come on, Jake." That was Mary. He noticed that Paige hadn't said anything. She only watched, her expression unreadable.

"I've taken the trophy the last five years," Frank said. "Might be interesting to have some new competition. It's been a long time, Jake."

Meeting Frank's eyes, Jake was suddenly sixteen again and determined to prove that there was nothing he couldn't do as well as or better than his best friend. The look in Frank's eyes was challenging, telling him that he remembered old times, too.

"Why not," Jake said, feeling reckless.

Paige stood near the front of the crowd, watching as the contestants lined up and the rules were explained. The contest was to be played in rounds, with only the top scorers going on to the next round, until it got down to the last two shooters. At that point, it would be the best two out of three rounds.

There were fifteen contestants to start with. Within two rounds, the field was narrowed down to five. Paige had eyes only for Jake. All of the contestants had grown up handling guns but there was something in the way Jake held the rifle . . . as if it was an extension of his arm. He didn't take as much time aiming as the other men, yet each of his shots were dead center.

As the field narrowed to four and then three, an odd hush came over the crowd. And then there were only two contestants left. Paige's teeth worried at her lower lip as she watched Frank load his rifle and bring it up to his shoulder. He took the first round and Jake took the second.

She could hear a muttering in the crowd as those who knew the history between the two men filled in those who didn't. Glancing across the crowd, she saw Josie watching, her hands clenched into fists at her sides, her mouth drawn tight. If Jake was aware of the tension building in the crowd behind him, it didn't show. His hands were steady as he loaded the rifle.

Paige was no longer the only one to notice the way he handled the gun, the calm way he fired off his shots. Suddenly, she had the disturbing thought that he'd be just as calm if it were a man standing out there and not just a paper target. She pushed the thought away. Sliding a look sideways, she could see Mary's eyes, wide and fascinated. There was a certain grimness in Martin's face. He could feel the tension in the crowd as well as she could.

Frank shot first, his shots neatly spaced and all in the black. Jake barely glanced at Frank's target. He lifted the rifle, set it against his shoulder and fired, all in one motion. The shots came so close together, they were one blast of sound.

There was dead silence as Jake set the rifle down. Paige wondered if she was imagining that there was something defensive in the set of his shoulders. No one moved or spoke as the target was brought in. From where she stood, Paige could see the center. There was one neat hole only slightly frayed around the edges. She felt a shiver run up her spine as she realized that he'd put all the bullets in a space that could have been covered by a quarter.

No one moved when the judges announced the winner. Jake turned slowly, his face completely expressionless and yet somehow communicating defiance as he let his gaze sweep the crowd. Paige suddenly thought of the boy he'd been, determined not to show anyone how much he was hurting.

Jake saw her start toward him, but Frank was there first, his expression rueful as he held out his hand.

"Damn fine shooting, Jake. Congratulations."

"Thanks." All Jake wanted to do was leave. Over Frank's shoulder, he saw Josie, her face white with fury. But then, everything about Jake seemed to infuriate her these days.

Paige slipped her hand through his arm and he turned, not caring if she could see how grateful he was for the interruption. She exchanged a few pleasantries with Frank that Jake barely heard.

He wondered how he could have been so stupid?

Paige finished her conversation with Frank and tugged on Jake's arm. The muscles under her hand were like iron. As they stepped into the crowd, space opened around them as people moved out of the way. She felt Jake's arm twitch but she kept her expression pleasant as if she were unaware of the fact that people were watching him much as they might have watched a lion who'd just been set loose in their midst.

It wasn't until they were back on the fairway that Jake spoke.

"I think—"

"I want some cotton candy," Paige interrupted, not in the least concerned about being rude. She knew what he thought. He thought he should go home, but she had no intention of letting him. "Mary, do you want some cotton candy?"

Mary, bless her, responded immediately, though she eyed Jake a bit uneasily. Paige dragged Jake to the cotton candy stand, thrusting a cone of the spun sugar into his hand. He looked at it as if he didn't know what to do with it but she didn't give him time to consider. Next came the merry-go-round. If he'd looked surprised to find himself eating cotton candy, he looked even more surprised to find himself sitting astride a garishly painted pony while tinny music blared out of a cracked speaker.

By the time the sun had gone down, Jake's expression was no longer so bleak. Paige rather ruthlessly insisted that he have fun. She hadn't allowed him time to brood. By pretending that nothing untoward had happened, she made it impossible for him to dwell on the shooting contest.

Nibbling on her second batch of cotton candy, Paige watched Jake and Martin, who were discussing the relative merits of the stock cars that would soon be racing around the makeshift track. Mary was talking to another friend and Paige was momentarily alone, or at least as alone as she could be in a crowd of hundreds.

Her eyes narrowed on Jake. She'd never known a man like him before. And she was willing to bet she'd never meet anyone like him again. Her life had always fallen along safe pathways, as much through circumstance as choice.

But there was nothing safe about Jake.

He was the kind of man her mother had warned her about. He'd be gone with the summer sun. A wise woman would keep her distance. To get involved with him was to court heartache.

But if she took the safe path this time, she'd never forgive herself.

As darkness fell, the fair became a magical place. Everything took on added mystery as the lights came on, gilding the shabby canvas awnings, turning the rides into sparkling jewels of moving color.

It was nearing midnight when Paige pulled Jake toward the Ferris wheel. The narrow gondola seat put them thigh to thigh and it seemed only natural for Jake to put his arm around her as the wheel turned, lifting them upward. When they were at the very top, the wheel came to a halt.

Paige leaned back, letting her head rest on his shoulder. Below them, the fair was all movement and color. To their right, the town was a more subdued glitter.

"It's beautiful, isn't it?"

When he didn't answer, she tilted her head back until she could see his face. He wasn't looking at the view. His hand came up to cup her cheek and Paige let her eyes drift shut. It was a slow gentle kiss that seemed to ask for nothing yet drew a response from deep within her soul.

They drew apart as the Ferris wheel jolted into motion again. Paige let her head rest on his shoulder and wished they could stay just where they were forever.

Walking home in the warm summer night air, Jake found his footsteps slowing. For a little while, he'd almost managed to pretend that the last twenty years hadn't gone by. He'd tasted what it felt like to be young and innocent, with his whole life stretched out in front of him again. He was reluctant to let that fleeting innocence go.

Paige had forgotten to turn the porch light on and the porch was full of deep shadows where even the moonlight couldn't penetrate. As if viewing his actions from a distance, Jake saw his arms go around Paige's waist, turning her to face him.

Kissing her here, on the dark porch, was another piece of those long-ago summers. How many times he had kissed Josie good-night, knowing her parents were waiting inside, counting the seconds he lingered with their daughter.

But this wasn't Josie and he wasn't a boy. Paige was warm and pliant in his arms, her mouth parting under his, as if it were made for him alone. The feelings she aroused were nothing like what he'd felt twenty years ago.

His hand flattened on her back, pulling her closer as the kiss deepened, his mouth slanting across hers. He wasn't sure how they'd come to be inside, but the shadowy darkness of the hall enclosed them, wrapping them together even more intimately.

He pulled her T-shirt loose from her jeans, his hand finding the warm skin of her back. She tasted of cotton candy and heaven. His palm cupped her buttocks, drawing her upward so that she was cradled against his thighs. She sucked in a quick breath at the feel of him boldly pressed against her and then she seemed to melt against him, her fingers sliding into his hair, her tongue tangling with his.

They were halfway up the stairs before a tiny voice of reason could make itself heard above the pounding of his heart. And they were in the warm darkness of her bedroom before he could drag a coherent thought out of the desire that seemed to beat in his head.

"Paige." He dragged the name out, struggling to remember all the reasons he couldn't let this happen.

"Jake." She'd unbuttoned the first three buttons of his shirt and she bent to put her mouth to his chest.

He caught her shoulders, holding her a little away when all he wanted to do was crush her to him.

"Paige, this isn't a good idea."

"Hmm." She leaned into his hands, forcing him to support her full weight. Her fingers found another button and slipped it loose.

"I'm not a good man, Paige. I've done things you couldn't even imagine."

"That's okay." Her palm stroked across his chest, her fingers threading through the thick mat of hair there. Jake swallowed hard, trying to remember what he wanted to say.

"I'm leaving in the fall."

"I know." His shirt hung open and her fingers were busy unbuckling his belt.

"This can't be anything more than a summer affair."

"I know." The rasp of his zipper sounded loud in the quiet room.

"I don't want to hurt you." The words were hardly more than a whisper.

At last, she lifted her eyes to his face. The moonlight that spilled in through the open curtains caught in her eyes, making them deep pools of mystery.

"I'm not asking you for anything more than tonight, Jake."

She was asking for so much more than that, whether she knew it or not. Paige wasn't the sort of woman a man gave only one night.

She didn't move as he reached up to loosen her hair from its braid. It spilled over his fingers, pale as the moonlight, warm as her eyes. Her palms settled on his chest as he drew her closer.

With her, he felt whole again in a way he'd never known. In the end, he couldn't walk away, no matter how much he knew he should. He needed what she was offering to fill his emptiness.

With a groan that was half curse, he bent to catch her up in his arms. Her eyes were fixed on his as he carried her across the room. Bracing one knee on the mattress, he lowered her to the bed.

The moonlight filled the room with silvery brilliance, blurring the line between shadow and light. Their clothing seemed to melt away. Paige's skin was cool against the fever that burned inside Jake. But there was nothing cool in her response.

She burned for him, twisting against the sheets as he explored her slender body. When he finally rose above her, her skin was flushed and feverish, her eyes heavy with passion.

His mouth caught her gasp as his body claimed hers. She was surely made for him alone. Never had anything felt so right, so inevitable.

Somehow, in the taking, he was taken. Somehow, in the giving, she received.

And in the aftermath, they were both left trembling and fulfilled.

Chapter Nine

Downstairs, the clock chimed. Jake listened, counting the bells. Four o'clock in the morning. It would be dawn in another hour or two. Paige stirred and his arms tightened around her.

They hadn't talked after they'd made love. Somehow, words would have been an intrusion. She'd fallen asleep as naturally as if they'd been sharing a bed for years, her head on his shoulder, the fine silk of her hair splayed across his chest, like a delicate chain, binding him to her.

Jake brushed his cheek against the top of her head, feeling a sense of peace he thought he had no right to feel. It was as if this was something that had been destined to happen.

Only two more months of summer left.

His eyebrows drew together as the thought intruded on his consciousness. He didn't want to think about that. He didn't want to think about anything but the woman who slept so peacefully in his arms.

The woman he'd be leaving behind.

But he hadn't lied to her about that. She'd known from the start that he'd be leaving.

Did that make him feel any less guilty?

Outside an owl hooted, a lost, lonely sound that found an echo in his heart. He had the rest of the summer. He wasn't going to look beyond that. He buried his face in her hair, letting the gentle scent of it precede him into sleep.

PAIGE AWOKE SLOWLY. She couldn't remember the last time she'd felt so completely relaxed. Forcing her eyes open, she squinted at the bright sunshine that poured in through the open windows. Funny, she usually closed the curtains before she went to bed.

She started to turn onto her back but the arm across her waist tightened and there was a rumble of protest in her ear. Any traces of sleepiness vanished and she was instantly wide awake.

Jake.

He was lying against her back, his legs drawn up beneath hers, his body cupping hers. It suddenly seemed very important that she get up before he awakened. Considering what they'd shared the night before, it didn't seem possible that waking up with him could seem even more intimate, but it did.

She inched her legs toward the edge of the bed but when she tried to lift his arm, it tightened around her. She gasped as she suddenly found herself flat on her back, his wide shoulders looming over her. She had only a glimpse of his face before his mouth covered hers in a slow, bone-melting kiss.

She gave in without a struggle, her arms coming up to encircle his shoulders. The crisp hair on his chest teased her nipples into wakefulness just as his kiss was stirring all her nerve endings to life. He drew back slowly, examining her face with a look of such profound male satisfaction that she flushed.

"Good morning." His voice held an early-morning rasp that sent a shiver up her spine.

"Good morning." She wanted to slide toward the side of the bed but he had her neatly trapped between the bulk of his body on one side and his braced arm on the other.

"Are you all right?"

Her gaze flickered to his face and then away while she debated the proper answer to his question.

Was she all right? It probably depended on whom you asked. She'd just slept with a man she'd known for less than a month, a man who was going to walk out of her life at the end of the summer. There were those who would have said that she was definitely something less than all right.

"I'm fine," she mumbled, staring at the hollow at the base of his throat. She moved slowly toward the side of the bed again, grateful when he moved his arm, allowing her to sit up and swing her legs off the edge.

That left her with a new problem. Her clothes were on his side of the bed. And her robe was hanging in the closet, where it did her no good at all. She supposed that, were she more sophisticated, she could just get up and casually saunter across the room.

She felt the bed shift as Jake got out on the other side.

"I think we should talk."

Paige glanced over her shoulder and then jerked her eyes away again. He was standing there magnificently, unself-consciously nude.

She wanted to run her fingers over his chest.

She wanted to scuttle for the safety of the bathroom.

Most of all, she wanted to know how to handle this awkward situation.

"Here. Why don't you put this on." Jake must have sensed her confusion. Gratefully, Paige took the garment he handed her. It was the shirt he'd worn yesterday. The shirt she'd so methodically unbuttoned the night before. It smelled like Jake, warm and woodsy. It was like being wrapped in his arms again.

With it safely buttoned, she slid off the bed, tugging the tail down to midthigh. She heard the rasp of his zipper as he put on his jeans, so she was able to face him with reasonable composure.

He looked, she thought, so much like a buccaneer that she wouldn't have been surprised to see a cutlass in his hand. A night's growth of beard shadowed his jaw, complementing the black leather patch over his eye. His hair was tousled, as much from her fingers as from the pillow. Since she was currently clutching his shirt rather desperately around herself, he remained bare chested. His jeans were zipped but not buttoned and rode low on his hips. Her eyes followed the line of dark hair that shaded his abdomen and disappeared beneath his waistband. She quickly diverted her gaze.

"Paige? We should talk."

"About what?" She stared over his shoulder.

"About last night." He sounded puzzled by her behavior. She couldn't blame him. She was hardly the picture of calm sophistication he was probably accustomed to waking up beside.

"Can't it wait?" She sidled around to the end of the bed. The bathroom door was so close. She could lock herself in there until she came to terms with last night. Like maybe for a year or two.

Jake caught her before she'd taken two steps. There was gentle but implacable strength in the arm that swept around her waist. Paige cast one despairing look at the sanctuary of the bathroom before his chest blocked her view.

"Paige? Are you really all right?" There was such concern in his voice that she felt tears burn her eyes. She was acting like an idiot. She was a grown woman, for heaven's sake. She drew a deep breath, forcing her eyes up to his face.

"I guess I'm not very good at this. I'm a little nervous."

"I'm not surprised you're not good at it." Jake's face softened in a smile, his teeth gleaming white beneath the thick mustache. "Why didn't you tell me it was the first time for you?"

Her flush deepened until her cheeks felt as if they were on fire. "Does it matter?" she mumbled.

"Well, if I'd known, I might have taken more time, been more careful." He broke off, shrugging.

She realized suddenly that he was almost as uneasy about this discussion as she was. The knowledge made her feel much better.

"You didn't need to take more time or be more careful. I . . . You were wonderful."

"Then why are you trying to sneak away this morning?" He slid one hand into her hair.

"I guess I'm not sure what the protocol is," she admitted, letting her hands settle on his chest.

"Well, I'm no expert, but I think a kiss would be in order."

The teasing tone was a new side of him and Paige found the last of her tension draining away.

"But we already kissed," she pointed out demurely.

"That was a long time ago and it wasn't nearly enough." He was staring at her mouth as he spoke, his gaze hungry.

"Then I suppose we'll just have to do it again, won't we?" Her hands slid upward, her fingers slipping into the thick dark hair at the nape of his neck.

"I guess we will."

The last word was smothered against her mouth. Paige melted beneath his kiss, feeling her knees weaken as his tongue slid between her lips to tangle with hers. His mustache brushed across her upper lip, prickly and soft at the same time. When she remembered the way it had felt against her breasts the night before, she felt even weaker in the knees.

She wasn't sure what Jake had intended when he kissed her—probably only to relax the tension. But the minute their lips met, one tension simply became another. He broke off the kiss, drawing his head back to look at her. Paige could only guess at what he saw—a woman whose mouth was swollen, whose eyes were slumberous.

If she'd ever thought that passion was a thing best experienced in the dark, Jake was proving that daylight could be just as potent. She rose up to meet his kiss, her breasts crushed against his chest, her mouth hungry.

Jake's hand slid under the loose tail of her shirt, his fingers splayed over her derriere as he lifted her up, until the rigid length of his desire was pressed against her.

Paige murmured approvingly, her hands sliding over the muscles of his back. She'd never have believed it possible, but she wanted him even more now than she had the night before. It was as if last night had only stoked the fires of the attraction between them.

Jake was lowering her to the bed, his hands seeking out the buttons that held her shirt together, when the front door opened and closed with a bang.

"Paige?"

"Josie." Paige breathed the name out, her wide eyes fixed on Jake's face.

"Maybe she'll go away."

"Paige? Are you still asleep?"

The sound of Josie's footsteps on the stairs was like a bucket of cold water, dousing their passion. Jake straightened abruptly. Paige jerked upright, scrambling off the bed, trying to find the jeans she'd discarded the previous night. But there was no time. She yanked at the tail of Jake's shirt, wishing it covered her to her ankles, instead of just her thighs.

"Paige?" Josie pushed open the door as Paige turned to face it. Jake turned his back and Paige felt wild color rise in her cheeks when she realized the reason. Not that it would have made any real difference. It was blatantly obvious that they'd just climbed out of bed, and just as obvious that they'd been about to climb back into it.

Josie took one step into the room before the scene before her registered. Paige didn't need a camera to know what her sister saw. She saw Jake, shirtless, his back half turned, his hair tousled from her fingers. Herself, wearing nothing but a man's shirt, her mouth swollen, her face flushed and her hair tossed in wanton disarray over her shoulders. And behind them was the rumpled bed.

The picture could have been titled "Caught in the Act."

For the space of several slow heartbeats, no one spoke. Throwing a wild look at Jake, Paige wondered just what Miss Manners would suggest as an appropriate greeting for such a situation.

"Josie. Hello."

As greetings went, it could have been more original. It hardly mattered since she didn't think her sister heard it anyway.

Josie's eyes went from Jake to Paige, the color slowly draining from her face. She threw one look at the bed and then turned and fled as if the hounds of hell were at her heels.

Paige listened to the sound of her sister's shoes clattering down the stairs. Then she heard the front door slam shut. Out in the street, a car engine roared to life and then the car took off from the curb at a dangerous speed.

The silence left behind in the bedroom was absolute. Paige stared at the doorway, desperately searching her mind for something clever and witty to say.

"I don't think she was happy to see us," she said at last.

"There's no reason for her to object," Jake said.

"No, of course not." But she wondered. In the instant before Josie had rushed out of the room, she'd looked absolutely shattered, almost like a woman betrayed.

The mood had definitely been spoiled and Jake didn't try to stop her as she gathered up her robe and went into the bathroom with a mumbled excuse about getting ready for work.

When she came back out, he was gone. She was just as glad. She needed a little time before she saw him again, time to come to terms with the probable foolishness of what she'd done.

She dressed and walked to work, opening up the library automatically.

The carnival folk would be packing up their rides and tents, preparing to go on to the next town. She'd watched them move one year but it had spoiled all the magic to see the mechanical side of it all. Maybe it would have been better if she'd seen a little less magic and a little more reality last night, she thought, carefully shelving Thoreau with the cookbooks.

Did that mean she regretted last night?

Now there was the sixty-four thousand dollar question. She frowned at a book of plays by Euripides before shelving it next to a children's picture book.

No, she didn't regret last night. She was remarkably clear on that, considering how fuzzy the rest of her thinking was. She'd been too careful for too long. The time had come to take a few risks.

"So you started out with a big risk," she muttered to herself, shelving a car repair manual among the modern poetry.

Well, she'd never been inclined to wade the shallow end. She either stayed out of the water or jumped in up to her neck. And this had been quite a leap.

The question was: What did she do now?

It was a question she debated most of the day. Usually, she was just as glad that the library saw so little business. But today, she could have done with hordes of children demanding help with their term papers. Since school was out, this wasn't likely to occur. Today, there was too much time to think.

By the end of the day, she was no closer to knowing what her next move should be than she had been when she'd slipped out of the house that morning, grateful that she didn't have to face Jake again.

When she got home, she could tell Jake was in the kitchen. She could smell garlic and ginger, which told her that he was probably cooking something oriental. She slipped off her shoes in the hall, setting them with military precision at the foot of the stairs.

Jake's back was to her when she stepped into the kitchen. He was wearing a pair of worn black jeans that molded his thighs in a way that was positively sinful and a blue T-shirt the color of his eyes.

Looking at the way the T-shirt stretched across his back, Paige's fingers curled with the remembered feel of hard muscle and warm skin. She must have made some sound because he turned away from the counter, his gaze finding her instantly.

He didn't come toward her and she realized he was uncertain of her reaction. A lock of hair had fallen over his forehead, making him look touchingly vulnerable. He reached up to adjust the eye patch and Paige found all of her doubts melting away.

"Hi."

"Hi," he said quietly, still trying to determine her mood. "If you're hungry, there's plenty."

"I'm starving." She reached up and loosened the top button of her blouse. Jake's gaze dropped to her hand as the next button opened and then the next. He reached behind him and very carefully set down the knife he'd been using to slice mushrooms.

Paige's blouse was open to the waist now and she began to tug it loose from her skirt. Her stomach tightened in anticipation as he started across the kitchen toward her.

He would be leaving at the end of the summer but that was two months away. She'd never know another man like him. Even if it was only for a little while, she was going to enjoy every moment they had.

IT HAD BEEN a rather rocky start to her first affair but Paige wasn't complaining. Jake was a marvelous lover and she didn't need prior experience to know that. He mapped her body with his hands, finding just the way to touch her to reduce her to quivering need.

But it wasn't a one-way street. He neither wanted nor expected her to be passive. Tentatively, at first, Paige explored the planes and angles of him. He was all lean muscles and sinew. And scars.

"What happened here?" She traced her fingers over a thin white scar on his shoulder.

"A bar fight in Hong Kong."

"And this one?" She traced an indentation low on his side.

"Someone was target practicing in Beirut," he said absently, more interested in the way the early-morning sunlight caught in her hair.

"And you were the target?"

"Only because I happened to be in the way."

"You seem to have been in the way a lot," she said, frowning. "Do all couriers get so banged up?"

"Only the clumsy ones." He ran his hand down her bare back.

"What about this scar? What happened here?" She traced her finger over a long, puckered scar on his upper thigh.

"Now, that was a bad one," he said. He sounded so solemn that she looked up into his face, wondering if she'd touched off a bad memory.

"What happened?" Any number of grim scenarios were spinning through her imagination, each more graphic than the one before. Her eyes were wide and full of sympathy.

Jake pulled the corner of his mouth down and shook his head as if not sure whether to tell her the gory details.

"Barbed wire," he said. Paige bit her lower lip, images of capture and torture gleaned from late-night movies, floating through her head.

"Oh, Jake."

He shook his head again. "I was lucky really. He was coming after me with a shotgun."

"You could have been killed."

"Well, not really," he said, seeming to consider it. "I'm pretty sure he just had it loaded with buckshot. I got that scar climbing over old man Grimes's fence."

"Old man Grimes?" It took Paige a moment to transform the images of swarthy torturers to the withered old man who had a farm and orchard operation on the south end of town. "Old man Grimes?" she repeated, her voice climbing.

"Yeah. I was fifteen. He had the best apples but he wasn't really crazy about having them stolen. Frank and I climbed through the fence but we barely had a chance to grab more than a couple of apples before Grimes came charging out of the house with a shotgun."

"You and Frank."

"We took off running. It's amazing what the sight of a shotgun can do for your speed."

"And you tore up your leg going over the fence?"

"Like I said, I was lucky. Frank wasn't quite as fast and he got a seat full of buckshot. Couldn't sit down for a week. Ouch!"

She'd found the tender skin along his side and had pinched him. "It's a shame you didn't get your rear end peppered with a little buckshot. It would have served you right."

"You're a hard woman," he complained, lifting her so that she lay on top of him.

She smiled down at him, shifting subtly, feeling his response. "And you're a hard man, Jake Quincannon. Just the way I like you."

His mouth smothered her smile and she forgot all about scars and old men with shotguns.

THERE WAS NO TALK of commitment, no promises made between them, no words of love spoken. Paige tried not to think about the end of the summer. She'd deal with it when it arrived. She knew he would be taking a piece of her with him when he left, but she wasn't going to think about that now.

As the days passed, it was hard for Paige to remember a time when Jake hadn't been a part of her life. Everything seemed so much sharper, so much more interesting now. It was as if she'd spent her whole life waiting for him to come along and shake her out of her cocoon.

And there was a change in Jake, too. She didn't think it was her imagination that some of the tension had drained from him. He smiled more often. And though he was careful not to let her see him without the eye patch, he didn't feel the need to constantly make sure it was in place, something she knew he did when he was feeling uneasy.

There was only one real cloud in the sky and that was Josie.

Despite the fact that they lived in a small town, where it was hard to turn around without bumping into someone you knew, Paige and Josie usually saw very little of each other. Josie was busy with various committees and with trying to find ways to advance Frank's career. She had her eye on politics, though Paige didn't think Frank's eye was turned in the same direction.

Suddenly, Josie was finding excuses to drop by the library almost daily. Paige watched this development somewhat warily. She knew her sister well enough to know that Josie never did anything without a reason.

The first time Josie dropped by was two days after she'd burst in on Jake and Paige. Paige assumed she'd come to harangue her for getting involved with Jake, but Josie made no mention of the incident. She chatted about happenings around town and what Beth was doing. It was right before she left that Jake's name came up.

"You know, I was furious when Jake won the shooting contest at the fair the other day."

"Were you?" Paige continued sorting file cards, her hands steady.

"Yes. It was silly of me, really. It's just that I hated to see Frank lose. It's so important to him, you know."

Paige didn't know any such thing but she mumbled something noncommittal. She had the feeling that Josie was finally getting around to the real reason for her visit, but she still couldn't tell what it was.

"As soon as Jake entered, I knew poor Frank didn't have a chance."

"It seems to me that Frank held his own."

"Oh, yes, he did all right." Josie smoothed one hand over her bone-colored purse, her expression pensive. "But it was easy to see that, whatever Jake has been doing all these years, he's had a lot of experience with guns."

"Was it?" Paige questioned vaguely, snapping one file drawer shut and opening another. She pulled cards out at random.

"You know, when we were younger, Jake used to take me target shooting with him. You were hardly more than a baby then, you wouldn't remember."

Josie didn't notice the way Paige's eyebrows rose at that. Generally, Josie preferred to reduce the number of years between them, not increase them.

"I wasn't crazy about it. All that noise, you know. But Jake would just beg me to go with him and I usually gave in. It was so important to him to have me there. Really, he could hardly stand having me out of his sight."

"That's nice," Paige said, as if she hadn't heard a word Josie had said. Out of the corner of her eye, she saw Josie's mouth tighten with irritation. She stood abruptly.

"You seem to be very busy," Josie snapped.

Paige looked up as if half-surprised to see that Josie was still there. "I'm sorry, Josie. I didn't mean to ignore you. All this paperwork, you know." She gestured apologetically in the direction of her nearly empty desk.

She watched Josie leave before leaning back in her chair. It wasn't hard to see what Josie's game was. Dog in the manger had always been one of her favorite diversions. She didn't want Jake but it galled her to think that someone else might have him. Particularly when that someone else was her little sister.

No, the game wasn't hard to recognize. But there *was* a grain of truth in what she'd said. Jake *had* been madly in love with her. Paige had been old enough to see that. But Jake's reasons for coming back had nothing to do with any old feelings for Josie. He'd told her that and she believed him.

Didn't she?

"THIS IS ABSURD. No one picnics in front of an empty fireplace." Jake looked at Paige across the blanket she'd spread on the living-room floor.

"You have to use your imagination. It's ten degrees outside and we've got a roaring fire in the fireplace."

"It's the middle of summer. You're wearing shorts. And just the thought of a roaring fire makes me sweat."

Despite his complaints, Jake made no move to get up. Paige grinned at him across the remains of a cold chicken dinner.

"I could think of more interesting ways to make you sweat," she suggested.

"Oh yeah?" He raised one eyebrow, a half smile tugging at the corners of his mouth.

"Yeah."

She'd only just begun her demonstration when the sound of quick footsteps on the porch interrupted them. Jake heard it first and lifted his mouth from hers. She murmured a protest, her hands tightening on his shoulders.

"There's someone on the porch," he muttered, levering himself upward.

"Whoever it is, tell them we're busy." Paige's eyes held an erotic slumberous promise.

"I will." He dropped a quick hard kiss on her mouth before pushing himself to his feet. He grabbed his shirt, shrugging into it on the way to the door, stopping to button his jeans. Whoever it was, he had every intention of getting rid of them quickly.

"If you don't leave me alone, I'm going to scream and wake up the whole neighborhood." He recognized Beth's voice, anger and a touch of fear making it louder than usual.

He jerked open the door in time to see her trying to push away the lank-haired youth she'd been with at the fair. At the sound of the door, the boy released her. He backed off a step when he saw Jake's figure looming in the doorway.

"Is there a problem here?" Jake asked, his eyes never leaving the boy's face.

"Nothing but the fact that Billy thinks I owe him . . . things just because he's taken me out." Beth's voice was shaky.

"Did he hurt you?"

Billy blanched at the cold menace in Jake's tone.

"I'm all right." Beth's voice steadied, Jake's presence giving her confidence.

"Shall I beat him to a pulp?"

Billy backed off another step, his pale eyes never leaving Jake's face.

"I didn't hurt her," he whined. "She thinks she's too good to put out."

Jake stepped onto the porch, threat in every line of his large frame. With a terrified squeak, Billy broke and ran, tripping down the steps and nearly falling flat on his face before gathering himself up and sprinting down the walk.

"You want me to go after him?"

"No, that's all right." Billy's rattletrap car peeled away from the curb as if it were the starting line of a race.

"Are you okay?" Jake asked as the taillights disappeared around the corner.

"I'm okay." She startled him by turning and putting her arms around his waist, pressing her face into his chest in a quick hug. "Thank you, Jake."

"You're welcome." He patted her back awkwardly.

"What's wrong?" He was grateful for Paige's interruption.

Paige led the way into the kitchen, making a pot of tea while Beth talked. She seemed more angry than hurt.

"You know what's so infuriating?" Beth looked across the table to where Jake and Paige were sitting, her eyes dark blue with emotion.

"What?" Paige asked. She lifted her teacup. Her other hand rested on Jake's thigh beneath the table in a gesture so casual he wasn't even sure she was aware of it.

"Mom was right when she said he was a creep." Beth sounded so gloomy that Jake had to restrain a smile. Paige glanced at him, her eyes laughing.

"It is depressing to find your parents can be right sometimes," she agreed solemnly.

"You can laugh if you want," Beth said, not in the least fooled. "But you know how Mom is when she's right about something like this. It doesn't happen often but she never lets you forget when it does. I'll be hearing about this for the rest of my life. She'll use this as an excuse to vet every boyfriend I have from now until doomsday.''

"I wouldn't worry too much about it. You're leaving for college pretty soon. Not even Josie is going to fly to Berkeley to investigate your love life."

"Wanna bet?"

Beth lingered over her tea, telling them that if she went home early, she'd have to explain what had happened and she just didn't want to face that tonight.

Despite the somewhat inopportune timing of her interruption, Jake didn't mind Beth's presence. He hadn't had much experience with nineteen-year-old girls over the last twenty years but she seemed to have more common sense than he'd have expected from someone so young.

She was taking Billy's loss philosophically, without any breast-beating or wailing about a blighted life. He didn't doubt that she was hurt, but she seemed to have a firm grasp on the fact that this was hardly the end of the world.

Oddly pragmatic, considering her mother's character. But Frank had always been a sensible sort. She must take after her father, he decided.

It was approaching eleven o'clock when Beth decided it was late enough for her to go home without having to explain herself. Jake took her home on the Harley. Beth was young enough to enjoy the ride, despite the recent blow to her love life.

He brought the bike to a halt at the end of the driveway so that no one would hear its distinctive roar, forcing explanations Beth didn't want to give just yet. Balancing the big bike, he reached back a hand to help her slide off.

Feeling her eyes on his, Jake turned his head. In the moonlight, she looked very young and very serious.

"I want to thank you for what you did tonight, Jake."

"It wasn't much. I don't think he'd have hurt you, even if I hadn't been there."

"Maybe not. But it was sure nice to have you there."

She hesitated and Jake had the feeling that she was debating whether or not to say something more. He waited, his feet braced on either side of the bike. The night air was slightly cool. Paige was waiting for him. There was a pleasant sense of anticipation in the knowledge of that.

"Are you in love with Paige?"

The question startled him. It startled him even more to realize that the answer wasn't as easy to give as he'd have liked.

"I don't think that's something I want to discuss with you," he said carefully.

"I know it's none of my business. But Paige is really special. I don't want to see her get hurt."

"I don't, either."

Beth hovered a moment longer, as if wanting to say something more. Perhaps she decided she'd pushed her luck as far as she dared. With a mumbled good-night, she ran up the driveway toward the big house.

Jake watched her go, his eyebrows hooked together in a frown. He'd told her the truth when he'd said he didn't want to see Paige get hurt.

The question was: Was it already too late to prevent it?

Chapter Ten

August slipped slowly, inexorably by. Paige avoided looking at calendars and refused to think about summer's end. It didn't seem possible that there'd been a time when Jake hadn't been a part of her life, and she wasn't going to think about a time when he wouldn't be again.

They talked of anything and everything. Anything but his leaving and everything but the future.

She told herself it was enough and almost managed to believe it.

She submerged herself in the present, aware in the back of her mind, that she was creating warm memories to hold against what might be a very cold winter.

The only thorn on the rose of her days was Josie's niggling little comments about how special she and Jake had been together, how much he'd loved her, how he'd sworn to always love her. For the most part, Paige could ignore her remarks, recognizing them for the barbs they were. But doubts lingered in the back of her mind.

If she and Jake had some spoken commitment, she might have asked him, might have let him reassure her.

But that wasn't the case and she told herself she was being a fool to let any of Josie's mud stick at all.

She wasn't going to worry about anything beyond living life to the fullest. After all, the here and now were all the guarantees anyone had.

Her here and now was Jake. The future could go hang.

"SORRY I'M LATE." Mary slipped into the booth, settling herself into a seat across from Paige. Her short dark hair was tumbled around her face and her cheeks were flushed from hurrying.

"That's okay. I was just enjoying the ambience while I waited."

"Ambience? In Maisie's? You must be delirious. Or in love." The last was said with what Mary believed to be a casual air.

"Maybe it's the heat," Paige suggested, pretending that she hadn't noticed the innuendo.

Ethel, Maisie's only waitress, appeared beside the table, her lavender hair immaculately coiffed in a style that hadn't changed in thirty years.

"You girls ready to order?"

They both ordered hamburgers, fondly labeled a "speciality" on the plastic-covered menu. In truth, it had been so long since anyone had ordered anything but a hamburger, it was possible the cook would have been thrown into confusion if something different had been requested.

Ethel lingered after writing down the order. "I hear Jake Quincannon's been staying at your place, Paige."

Paige saw Mary roll her eyes but she kept her tone pleasant.

"Yes, he has."

"Don't see much of him around town."

"I guess he hasn't had much reason to spend time in town."

"I saw him when he came in that first day, you know," Ethel said, fussing with the salt and pepper shaker, arranging them just so in the metal holder that was attached to the edge of the table.

"So I heard from several different people." Ethel gave Paige a sharp look, wondering if Paige was implying that she gossiped, which the good Lord knew she certainly didn't. But Paige's expression was blandly pleasant, not a hint of sarcasm to be read.

"I knew him right away," she continued importantly. "It's been twenty years but I knew him right off. Couldn't be anybody else with that wicked look about him. He looked just the same when he was a boy. Younger, of course, but that same look. Always looked like he was up to no good."

"That's funny. I don't remember Jake getting into much trouble when he lived here before." Paige's tone remained even but her eyes had taken on a chill.

"You're too young to remember much about him. He was trouble, all right. Clean through. I swear, I used to pity poor Margaret havin' a son like that."

"Really? Just what did Jake do that was so terrible?"

"It wasn't what he did so much," Ethel said. "It was the way he looked. Sort of arrogant and know-it-all."

"So because you didn't like the way he looked, you labeled him a troublemaker?"

"Well, it wasn't just that," Ethel said, not sure how she'd come to be on the defensive.

"Then he *did* do something specific?" Paige pressed ruthlessly.

"Well...I...Not that I recall right off the bat," Ethel stammered.

"I didn't think so." Paige's smile would have done justice to a shark. "Would you add a side order of fries to that order, please?"

Ethel nodded, grateful for a chance to retreat.

"You were a little hard on her, weren't you?" Mary asked.

"I'm tired of hearing how bad Jake was, when not one person can substantiate it."

"You know," Mary said carefully, "some people would say that where there's smoke there's fire."

"And it's probably just a smudge pot. Look, I'm not saying he was a saint, but the way the people in this town act, you'd think he was Dracula or something."

She leaned back as Ethel set two milk shakes in front of them, then scurried off without a word.

"I think you've scared her," Mary said, reaching for her chocolate shake.

"Good. She's the most notorious gossip in town."

"So, how is Jake?"

"He's fine." Paige stirred her milk shake with her straw.

"I haven't seen him around and Martin hasn't mentioned seeing much of him. Not since the fair."

"He's been doing a lot of work around the house. He seems to be enjoying himself and I'm not going to complain. The window in the kitchen hasn't worked since Dad died and he fixed the leak in the basement."

"Paige." Mary fixed her friend with a worried look that sat oddly on her round face. "You're not falling in love with him, are you?"

"I haven't decided yet," Paige said in a flip tone.

"I know it's none of my business but I don't want to see you get hurt. And if he's leaving at the end of the summer, it would be a big mistake to fall in love with him. I'm not saying he's not a great guy and all. Although I've got to be honest and say he makes me kind of nervous. But it's just not a good idea to go falling in love with someone you know is leaving in a month."

"Mary." Paige stretched her hand across the table, catching her friend's fingers, which were mutilating a straw wrapper. "I appreciate your concern."

"It's just that you're my best friend and I want to see you happy."

"That makes two of us," Paige said lightly. "I'm not even sure what I feel about Jake. But he's a good man and I—care—about him. And I'm not going to worry about the end of the summer till it gets here. Now, tell me how the new book is going."

Mary was willing to let herself be distracted and the conversation turned to other things. Paige listened somewhat absently to the problems Mary was having with a recalcitrant character, who simply didn't want to do any of the things she thought he should do.

When they said goodbye in front of Maisie's, thick gray clouds were scudding across a steely sky. It looked as though the rain that had been threatening for two days was finally going to arrive.

Paige brushed her hair back over her shoulders. She slipped her hands into the pockets of her jeans, and considered her options. The library was only open half days during the month of August, so the afternoon stretched out in front of her. She could go to Harl's Department Store. Mary had said that they had received a new shipment of shoes. She could go to the little park behind the courthouse and feed the ducks.

Or she could go home and see what Jake was up to.

JAKE WIPED the back of his hand across his forehead, brushing away beads of sweat. Glancing out the garage door, he could see heavy clouds. They seemed to press down on the land, holding the heat to the ground like a thick blanket. It had clouded up like this the last two afternoons but it hadn't rained. There was a good chance the storm would break this afternoon.

With a last glance at the sky, he turned his attention once more to the maple table he'd spent the morning sanding. It had been sitting on the back porch, layers of grime and a scuffed finish hiding the beauty of the wood. When he'd mentioned it to Paige, she'd shrugged and told him it had been there ever since she could remember.

He wasn't sure just why he'd decided to refinish it. Woodworking had never been a hobby of his. But it had seemed a shame to leave the warm beauty of the wood hidden. And maybe he liked the idea that, when he left, he'd leave something behind that was in better shape than it had been.

Running his hand over the smooth grain, he half smiled. It had been a long time since he'd spent time doing something like this, something simple and productive. There was no hidden subtext, no need to look for deeper meanings. The wood responded to his efforts in a gratifyingly straightforward way.

Shaking his head, he picked up the sanding block and replaced the worn sandpaper with a finer grade. He was really losing it when he began seeing the meaning of life in a simple refinishing job.

He ran the sanding block over the table top, using long straight strokes, smoothing the grain. The temperature hovered in the eighties and the humidity felt almost as high. He'd discarded his shirt earlier and his torso gleamed with a fine sheen of sweat.

"I don't remember you wanting to be a carpenter."

Jake cursed as he came down too hard on the sanding block, one corner digging a shallow groove into the wood. Absorbed in his task, he hadn't heard Josie's approach. He straightened, his hand automatically checking the eye patch as he turned and looked at her.

She was standing just inside the door, wearing a pair of tailored ivory linen slacks and a blue silk blouse that looked completely out of place in the cluttered garage.

"Josie," he said flatly, letting her name serve as a greeting. "Paige isn't home."

"I know." She came farther in, running her fingers over a rusty bike frame. "This used to be my bike. Remember how I'd ride out to the lake to meet you?"

"I remember how you used to complain about the road being too rough."

Josie slanted him an unreadable glance, wandering around the edge of the garage, touching things here and there, her expression pensive. Jake watched her warily. As far as he knew, Josie thought he was one short step above an ax murderer. She'd avoided him quite successfully all summer. In fact, he hadn't even seen her since the morning she'd walked in on him and

Paige. So if she knew Paige was gone, why was she here?

"We had some good times, didn't we, Jake?"

"I suppose so."

"Do you ever think about those times?"

"Not much."

Her mouth tightened for a moment before she seemed to make a conscious effort to relax it into a soft smile.

"I think about them." Her meanderings had brought her around the table until she stood in front of him. Now she looked up at him, her expression wistful. "Those were some of the best times of my life."

"Were they?" She was too close but there was no way he could move away without making it obvious. She had him neatly trapped. He reached for his shirt, feeling suddenly naked.

"We were so much in love. I don't think you ever get over your first love completely."

"It was a long time ago, Josie. We were kids." He shrugged into his shirt.

"We were old enough to know we loved each other. Old enough to make love."

"It doesn't take any maturity to do that," he said dryly, wishing she'd back off.

"Don't you sometimes wonder what it would have been like if you hadn't gone away, if I hadn't married Frank?"

"Not really." He didn't care if he was less than tactful. He didn't like the direction this conversation was taking.

"I do. We were so good together, Jake. You remember how it was between us. You couldn't get enough of me."

"I was a nineteen-year-old boy, Josie. I hate to be blunt, but nineteen-year-old boys don't require a great deal of emotional commitment as a prerequisite for sex."

Something flashed in her eyes, something very close to hatred but it was gone so quickly he thought he'd imagined it.

She moved closer. He'd already retreated until his back was pressed against a pile of boxes. Unless he darted around her like a frightened rabbit, there was nowhere left to go.

"It was more than that, Jake. We were in love. We had something special."

"It was twenty years ago, Josie."

She set her hands against his chest, bare between the open sides of his shirt. Her eyes were full of soulful nostalgia as she looked up at him.

"Something so intense doesn't just die. Isn't there still a spark there?"

Looking at her, Jake found it hard to remember why he'd once thought himself so passionately in love with her. So in love that he'd wanted to kill his best friend over her. Had she been this shallow even then?

She was Paige's sister, he reminded himself. They might not be close but Paige would probably prefer it if he used a little tact, rather than just shoving the woman away.

"Josie, it was a very long time ago. We were different people then. Even if that weren't the case, Paige and I are . . . involved."

It seemed such an anemic word to describe his relationship with Paige. He might as well not have spoken for all the effect it had.

"I know you still want me, Jake." Before he could prevent it, she threw her arms around his neck and pressed her mouth to his.

Jake jerked back as if she were an adder. His hands caught her shoulders, none too gently, thrusting her away. Josie stared at him, reading the revulsion he couldn't hide. An ugly flush mantled her cheeks. Her mouth tightened into a pinched line.

"You can't possibly prefer *her* to me," she said, spitting the words out.

The light dawned and Jake wondered how he could have been so stupid that he hadn't seen it from the start. This wasn't about him. It was about Paige. She didn't really want him at all. She just couldn't stand the thought that he was sleeping with Paige, not out of any lingering feelings for him or because she was worried about her sister. She simply didn't want anyone else to have something that she'd once considered hers.

He didn't even try to hide the contempt he felt. "Paige is ten times the woman you ever hoped to be, Josie."

Outside, thunder rumbled. Fat drops of rain began to fall as the storm broke at last. Josie stared at him, fully aware of his contempt. Her angry flush faded, leaving a pallor broken only by her carefully applied rouge, now ugly steaks of color on her ashen face.

Never in her life had she lost anything to Paige. *She'd* been the golden girl, the one their parents had loved first and best. *She'd* been prom queen. *She'd* married well. *She* had a position in society. It wasn't possible that anyone could prefer Paige to her. Paige, with her casual clothes and carelessly styled hair. Paige, who'd rather read a book than attend a party.

Jake read the emotions flickering across her face. Disbelief, shock, rage. She simply couldn't believe that he would reject her. She'd probably thought he'd be grateful that she'd condescend to offer herself to him.

"Paige will be home soon. I suggest you leave before she arrives."

He pushed past her without waiting for a response. Rain splattered his shoulders as he crossed the short distance to the house. The screen door banged shut behind him. Stripping off his shirt on his way upstairs, he headed straight for the shower. He felt dirty in a way that had little to do with the sweat he'd worked up sanding the table.

Josie's perfume seemed to cling to his clothes, the feel of her hands still lingered on his chest. He pulled off his jeans and turned on the shower with a wrenching motion. All he wanted was to wash away the smell and feel of Josie from his skin.

PAIGE PUSHED OPEN the front door, pausing to shake the rain from her hair before stepping into the hall. Luckily, she'd been almost home before the rain really started to come down.

"Jake?"

She shut the door behind her, tilting her head as she listened for a response. The garage door was open and the Harley parked just inside, so she knew he was home. She was about to call again when she heard the pipes bang as the shower was shut off too quickly.

Grinning, she started up the stairs. It would be fun to surprise him. What better way to spend a rainy afternoon than in bed? She took the last half of the stairway two steps at a time.

She already had her fingers on the buttons of her blouse as she pushed open the bedroom door. She came to a dead stop, feeling as if she'd just been kicked in the gut.

Josie started up from the bed, naked to where the sheet draped across her waist. Her clothing lay tossed over a chair. Her usually immaculate hair was tousled.

"Paige!" She looked the very picture of guilt as she sat there in the middle of the bed.

The bed where she and Jake had made love only that morning, Paige thought dully.

"Oh, Paige, I'm so sorry. Jake and I . . . I mean, we just . . ." Josie stammered. "I didn't mean for you to find out this way. I did try to warn you," she said, ending on a vaguely self-righteous note.

Josie's breasts were starting to sag, Paige noted. Had Jake noticed that? Of course, he'd probably had other things on his mind. How many times had Josie hinted at the possibility that she and Jake would get back together? Had it been going on all along?

Uneasy at the protracted silence, Josie drew the sheet up to her shoulders. She should say something, do something, Paige thought. But she couldn't seem to move, couldn't seem to think.

Somewhere deep inside her, someone was screaming.

Before she could break the spell that held her rooted to the spot, the bathroom door opened and Jake stood framed in the opening. Paige turned her head to look at him, her neck stiff.

He wore nothing but a towel draped low on his hips. Moisture beaded on his shoulders and caught in the mat of hair on his chest, making his skin gleam like damp copper. His hair was damp, falling into a heavy wave onto his forehead, touching the black leather patch over his left eye.

The other eye widened as he took in the scene before him—Josie in the midst of the tumbled sheets, Paige standing as if frozen in the doorway.

If Paige had been looking at Josie, she might have seen the fear that flared in her eyes when she saw Jake. But Paige looked only at Jake, such hurt and betrayal in her eyes that Jake felt the look as if it were a knife in his chest.

"Paige."

His voice was hoarse as he took a step forward, reaching out one hand.

The movement broke her frozen stance. Before he could stop her, she spun on her heel and ran from the room as if pursued by demons.

Jake whirled, snatching up his jeans from the bathroom floor and thrusting his legs into them.

"She'll never believe you," Josie said spitefully as he reached the bedroom door. The look of rage he shot her made her flinch.

"You'd better be gone when I get back." His quiet tone made the words more menacing than if he'd shouted threats.

He'd already dismissed Josie from his mind as he ran down the stairs. He'd heard the front door bang behind Paige seconds after she'd run from the room. He had to find her, had to explain that it wasn't what it had looked like.

Paige was halfway down the street when she heard the front door slam again. She was oblivious of the rain that was now coming down heavily, soaking her clothes and hair. She was blind to everything but the stabbing pain in her chest.

"Paige."

The sound of Jake's voice deepened the pain and she walked faster, trying to escape the hurt as much as the man who'd caused it. The concrete was cold beneath her bare feet. She'd kicked off her shoes when she'd gotten home, when she'd planned on creeping upstairs to surprise Jake. Wasn't it funny that she was the one who'd been surprised. A stone on the sidewalk bruised her heel but the pain only registered vaguely.

"Paige."

His hand came down on her shoulder, spinning her around to face him. She stared at his bare chest, refusing to lift her eyes any higher.

"It wasn't what you think."

She shrugged. "It doesn't matter," she said without emotion.

"Look at me." When she didn't move, Jake grabbed her by the shoulders, his fingers bruising with urgency. "Paige, look at me."

Hot tears slipped from the corners of her eyes to mingle with the cool rain. Jake gave her a quick shake, demanding her attention, demanding that she listen.

"Nothing happened, Paige."

"It's none of my business."

"Nothing happened," he repeated, trying to break through the wall of ice she was setting between them.

"There's no commitment between us."

"Dammit, Paige!" He shook her again, less gently this time. "I did not sleep with Josie."

"It's none of my business," she said again.

"Look at me, dammit." Frustrated, he grabbed her chin, forcing her face up until she had no choice but to meet his gaze.

"I did not sleep with Josie."

"It's none of my business."

"If you say that one more time, I'm going to shake you until your teeth rattle." Frustration deepened his voice to a rough growl. "I didn't sleep with your sister. It was a setup. Nothing happened between us except that she offered me her dubious charms and I turned her down. She was angry."

Paige blinked up at him, her lashes heavy with tears and rain. The tight pain in her chest eased enough to allow her to breathe. It sounded plausible. Josie *was* capable of almost anything when she was angry.

"Nothing happened?" she asked, her voice shaky.

His hand gentled her face, his thumb coming up to brush rain and tears from her cheeks.

"Nothing. Even if I wanted to sleep with another woman, do you really think I'd bring her to your home, to the bed we've shared?"

She bit her lip, wanting so desperately to believe him that she was afraid to let herself do so. With a sound that was perilously close to a sob, she stepped forward, wrapping her arms around his waist, her face pressed to his rain-drenched shoulder.

Jake held her that way for a moment before slipping his hand under her cheek, tilting her face up to his. His mouth was hard, almost frantic, and Paige responded with an urgency of her own. Her lips parted for him, welcoming the heavy thrust of his tongue, pressing her body close to his.

They stood there, locked in an embrace, oblivious of the pouring rain, indifferent to the fact that they were standing in the middle of the sidewalk, in full view of the neighbors, who were undoubtedly watching the scene with shocked interest.

Paige ran her hands up Jake's bare chest, slick with rain, her arms encircling his neck as he bent to sweep her up into his arms. Cradled against him, Paige had never felt more complete.

Jake kicked open the back gate, carrying her into the fenced backyard. Laying her beneath a huge old weeping willow, he followed her down, the weight of his body pressing her into the thick, soft grass. The grass was cool and damp beneath her back. Above her, Jake was all heat and fire.

Her hands slipped on his wet skin as his mouth twisted hungrily over hers. She shuddered as he unbuttoned her blouse, his palms cupping her breasts, his touch searing.

Hidden from prying eyes by the fence as well as the sheltering branches of the tree, they made love with explosive passion. They'd come so close to losing the fragile security they'd only just begun to find. Now they were reaffirming it with their bodies.

He might be hers only until the seasons changed, but until then, she knew he was hers alone.

Chapter Eleven

Never had summer flown by so quickly. The days slid one into another, rushing toward September. Paige refused to think beyond the next day. The future would come soon enough without her worrying about it. Jake was here for now and she'd never felt quite so alive. It was enough.

She was in love with him.

She'd never lied to herself before and she couldn't start now. She'd fallen deeply in love with a man who'd only come home for the summer. A man whose scars ran as deep as the emotions he tried so hard to hide. A man capable of both deep tenderness and unbridled passion.

When he left, he was going to take a vital piece of her with him.

But that was for the future. She'd deal with that time when she had to. For now, she was going to enjoy what they had without thinking about its ending.

BETH WAS a frequent visitor to the big old house. She came as much to see Jake as Paige. Since the night she'd broken up with Billy, she and Jake had developed an easy rapport. Jake had had little experience with girls Beth's age but he found she was good company.

When she had an afternoon off from the bank, she'd sometimes drop by and perch herself somewhere in the vicinity of whatever he was working on. Jake finally began putting her to work handing him tools and holding things for him.

She was as easy and natural as her aunt. If Beth wanted to know something, she saw no reason not to ask. On the other hand, she took no offense when he bluntly told her she was nosy. She grinned at him and said that she was practicing her interrogation techniques. If she was going to be an investigative reporter, she had to start somewhere.

Jake was surprised to find that he really liked her, despite her endless, disconcertingly blunt questions. Like Paige, you always knew where you stood with Beth.

Josie had suddenly become all but invisible. Jake saw her once or twice at a distance, but from the way she disappeared, he assumed she was no more anxious to run into him than he was to run into her. It wasn't so much what she'd done—or tried to do—that made him angry. It was the fact that she'd hurt Paige. He'd discovered he had a protective streak that Paige brought to the fore.

There was nothing all that complex about it, he told himself. He had a basic dislike of cruelty. Maybe because he'd seen so much of it. Josie hadn't wanted to accomplish anything with her little act beyond hurting Paige and, indirectly, Jake himself.

As August wound down, Jake felt a strange restlessness. Summer was almost over. The days were still long and hot but there was a feeling in the air that autumn was just around the corner. In a few short weeks children would be back in school.

He'd taken this summer to come home and find out who he was, to try and figure out where he wanted to go with the rest of his life, to make peace with his family.

His attempts to reconcile with his family had been less than successful. Each time he visited them, it seemed as if the tension only grew stronger. They didn't seem to have any common meeting ground, any way around the barriers that Time had set between them.

As for finding out who he was and what he wanted to do with his life, he couldn't say that he was much closer to resolution there, either.

All he'd really accomplished was that he'd added a new complication to his life in the form of a long-legged blonde who filled gaps in his life he hadn't even known were there.

He'd given little thought to what anyone else might think about his relationship with Paige. It had been a long time since he'd had any reason to wonder what other people thought. Despite the reminders he'd had, it hadn't occurred to him that he and Paige might be considered a hot topic for the gossip mill.

It had been a slow summer in Riverbend, with little to talk about. Oh, there was the standard gossip. Young Louise Denby had gotten herself into trouble with the Peters boy. Her parents were planning a hasty wedding and Mr. Denby was said to have oiled his shotgun in case of any reluctance on the groom's part.

Old Mrs. Murchison had decided to write her children out of her will again. It looked as if this time she might really do it. She'd called on Frank Hudson to draw up a new will leaving everything to a distant cousin. But she'd come close before and had always changed her mind. After all, blood was thicker than water.

One of the Fletcher twins had fallen out of the Baldwin's hayloft and landed right next to their milk cow, scaring her so badly her milk had dried up.

But this was the standard stuff any small town gossip mill was used to. Paige Cudahy and Jake Quincannon living in the same house together was something else entirely. She might call him a boarder if she wanted but everyone knew he was more than that. Hadn't Mrs. McCardle seen them kissing in the middle of the day? Bold as brass, standing there in the rain and him with no shirt on. And hadn't he picked her up and carried her off just like Rhett carrying Scarlett up the stairs.

There were a few who sighed and said they thought it was romantic but they were outnumbered by those who thought it was a crying shame that a sweet little thing like Paige was being so foolish. Jake Quincannon was trouble, sure as the sun came up every morning. Besides, everybody knew he was only home for the summer.

Just where was she going to be come September when he rode off on that motorcycle of his, leaving her alone? And Lord only knew if she'd been careful about protecting herself. What if she found herself in the family way? She had no menfolk to demand that Jake do the right thing by her. Besides, he could be long gone before she even found out.

Paige had always seemed so sensible. A bit reserved maybe, but not like that sister of hers, always thinking of herself. Sometimes it was the sensible ones who broke out and did the craziest things.

Though Jake had given little thought to what the local grapevine might be saying, he was brought nose to nose with it one afternoon late in August.

He and Pop and Martin had met for lunch, reminiscing about people and places. The old man had gone back to work, leaving Martin and Jake to linger over their cups of coffee.

"He was hell on wheels in his heyday," Martin commented as the door shut behind Pop's slightly stooped shoulders.

"He put the fear of God into me." Jake smiled nostalgically. "I don't know where I'd be if he hadn't taken it into his head to whip me into shape."

"Yeah. He sure had a way about him. When I came back, I drifted for a couple of years, in and out of one job and another. I kept a machine gun under the seat of my car, like I thought the VC were going to turn up in Idaho. Man, I was more than a few bricks short of a full load."

"Most of us came out of it missing a few gears," Jake said, his expression dark with memories.

"I guess. But at the time, I felt like I was the only one seeing demons in every shadow. I think Pop got tired of seeing me hanging around. He collared me one day and told me I was worrying my parents sick. He said if I was going to shoot myself, I ought to go ahead and get it over with. And if I wasn't going to shoot myself, I ought to damn well get on with my life."

"That sounds like Pop. The velvet hand in the iron glove." He twisted the adage with a smile.

"That's Pop. He taught me most of what I know about this job and I've always had the feeling that he didn't teach me *half* of what *he* knows. It was a crying shame when they forced him to retire. He lived for that job.''

There were only a few other customers in the bar. Two men played a desultory game of pool at the table in the center of the room. There were half a dozen customers lined up at the bar, drinking beer and talking.

The jukebox in the corner was playing a twangy tune that complained of cheating lovers and broken hearts. It was, perhaps, unfortunate that the song came to a close just when it did. The tinny music had served to drown out any sound more than a few feet away. As the song faded out, the conversation of the pool players was suddenly audible.

''Can't say I blame the guy. For years I've wondered what it would be like to have those legs wrapped around me. If I'd known she was open to suggestion, I might have done something about it.''

The speaker was a big man, six foot three and well over two hundred pounds. Years of drinking had put a paunch on him but it was backed by solid muscle. Jake barely heard what he said. It was barroom talk and of no interest to him. Until the man's friend spoke and he realized whom they were discussing.

''Wait till Quincannon leaves town, George. Maybe she'll be lonely then.''

In a flash Jake was out of his seat and halfway across the room, his approach as silent as it was lethal.

''You never can tell now,'' George said, chalking his cue, oblivious of the fact that he was teetering on the edge of disaster. ''Once she's had a taste of it, she ain't likely to be nearly so snooty.'' He set down the chalk.

"I wouldn't want to cross that Quincannon, though. He looks like a mean son of a bitch."

"He is," Jake said from less than two feet away.

George turned, his eyes widening when he saw who had spoken. He hadn't seen Jake and Martin in the corner booth or he would certainly have been more discreet in his choice of topics. But Jake didn't give him a chance to retract his words.

His left first buried itself in George's paunchy belly. As he doubled over, Jake's right fist caught him on the chin. He swung from near ground level and his fist carried the power of a mule's kick. George rocked back on his heels, his eyes rolling back in his head as he wobbled for a moment before collapsing onto the floor like a poleaxed ox.

Jake took a step toward George's friend but Martin's hand caught his arm, stopping him.

"That's enough, Jake. I'm sure Luke wants to apologize."

Luke wanted to apologize in the worst way for anything he'd said, anything he might have thought of saying or anything he might say at any time in the future that could possibly offend Jake in any way.

Jake nodded shortly, fighting back the urge to knock Luke's teeth down his throat. Any man who could talk about Paige like that didn't deserve to live. The fact that George lay unconscious on the floor at his feet only began to assuage the rage he'd felt when he'd realized whom they were talking about.

Martin continued to hold on to Jake's arm and could feel the tension in it. Jake let himself be herded outside. He knew if he stayed, there was likely to be bloodshed.

The sun was bright. Jake stood, his hands clenching and unclenching at his sides, surrounded by an almost visible aura of danger.

"George is a bit of a loudmouth," Martin said, reaching into his pocket for a pack of gum. Jake said nothing. Martin unwrapped a stick of gum with neat precision. "You know, you can't really expect to have an affair in a town this size without stimulating a bit of comment."

"We're not having an affair," Jake snarled, slanting the sheriff a look that held pent-up fury.

Martin folded the gum into his mouth, chewing it a few times to soften it. "Next weekend is Labor Day. End of summer." He glanced up at the sky as if he could see the inevitable change of seasons in the clear blue arc overhead. "You still leaving come fall?"

"I've no reason to change my plans," Jake said flatly, wondering if the words sounded as hollow to Martin as they did to him.

THE SMITH FAMILY had been having an annual end-of-summer barbecue for as long as most of the town's residents could remember. It was as much a part of the changing of the seasons as returning to school and digging out the woolens.

Jake hadn't planned on going. He remembered the barbecue from his childhood. A good portion of the town could be counted on to be in attendance, including his parents. Spending the afternoon under his mother's cool gaze was not exactly his idea of fun.

There was so little time left. Already, the nights were cooler, the days a little shorter. The end of summer was all but here and he still hadn't made any plans to leave. He kept thinking that there was no harm in staying just a few more days, just another week or two.

But there was harm. The longer he stayed, the more tangled up in Paige he became. It was already almost impossible to remember a time when he hadn't known her, a time when he hadn't awakened with her beside him. If he'd been another kind of man, led another kind of life, maybe things could have been different.

But he was what he was and the choices he'd made couldn't be changed. He should never have allowed himself to get involved with her. She was going to get hurt. He couldn't lie to himself about that, couldn't pretend that it was nothing more than a summer fling for her. She thought she was in love with him. She'd never said it but sometimes he could see it in her eyes.

She'd get over it, realize that he wasn't worth it. That was what he wanted. And if he told himself that a hundred more times, he just might begin to believe it.

His smile held an edge as he gave himself a last glance in the mirror. He stopped, caught by the image. He saw a man, long past his youth, all illusions beaten out of him by life. His hair held a scattering of gray. There were fine lines slanting away from his eyes and deeper lines bracketing his thick black mustache. He reached up, fingering the patch, the final touch to his battle-scarred appearance.

He wondered suddenly what Paige saw when she looked at him.

THE BARBECUE was already in full swing when Jake stopped the motorcycle at the foot of the driveway. The Smith house was a sprawling ranch, half a dozen miles from town. The driveway was already lined with pickups and cars, with more parked on the road in front. Jake slid the Harley into a narrow spot between a battered pickup and an even more battered sedan, nudging the kickstand into place as Paige hopped off.

She was wearing a pair of pale pink shorts that exposed the long, smooth length of her legs. When he'd first seen her in them, he'd had to suppress the urge to suggest that she put on something that was less revealing, like a nice full-length coat. Feeling possessive was something new to him and it wasn't a comfortable sensation.

"It looks like everybody got here before us," Paige said, linking her arm through his. Her other arm was wrapped around an enormous bowl of pasta salad, the same bowl that had jabbed him in the back all the way over. Jake thought it was a pity everyone hadn't already left before they got here.

But it wasn't as bad as he'd feared. True, when they'd first arrived, they were the cynosure of all eyes but it wasn't long before people's attention moved on to other things, like food and swimming in the inground pool Bob Smith had put in only this spring.

Even though Jake couldn't fade into the background, he could at least linger on the fringes of the gathering. He watched Paige talking to various friends and neighbors. She'd braided her hair again. The thick braid looked almost platinum in the sunlight. Jake wanted to wrap it around his hand and pull her to him.

He took a long draft from his beer, turning his gaze elsewhere. Josie was standing just across the patio from him, looking as out of place in her immaculately tailored slacks, silk blouse and high-heeled pumps as he felt. He noticed that she hadn't spoken to

Paige and Paige had made no effort to seek Josie out. Josie's eyes met his for a moment. Jake lifted his beer in mocking salute, admitting to a rather immature pleasure when she looked away, her mouth pinched.

"Are you going swimming, Jake?"

Beth darted up to him, her nose slightly sunburned, her blue eyes sparkling. She was wearing a bright pink terry sunsuit and he guessed she had a bathing suit underneath it.

"I don't think so."

"Too old and feeble?" she teased.

"Someone really should have spanked you more often," he complained, reaching out to tug a lock of her hair.

"People always say that when you touch a nerve. Come watch me dive."

Without waiting for an answer, she linked her arm through his, tugging him toward the pool. Jake saw a few speculative glances cast their way and, glancing over his shoulder, he saw Josie staring after them, her eyes dark with some emotion he couldn't read. She was probably worried about him contaminating her daughter.

"You really should come in, Jake," Beth coaxed. She stopped on the edge of the pool, reaching up to unzip the front of the sunsuit. Shimmying out of the modest terry cloth, she revealed a bikini of truly minuscule proportions. She laughed as Jake's eyes widened.

"Do you like it?"

"There's not enough of it to like," he said dryly.

"Isn't it great?" She waved to a girl already in the pool. "You sure you won't come in, Jake?"

Jake glanced at the pool, which was full of teen-agers whose average age was about sixteen. "I don't think so."

"If you'd just take your vitamins, you'd have more energy." She dodged the casual swat he aimed in her direction, laughing over her shoulder as she turned toward the pool. Jake half smiled, raising his beer to take a drink as he watched her.

The bikini was outrageous, of course, but she had the figure for it. A tiny strap cut across her back, the only covering until the scrap of fabric that barely stretched across her derriere.

The bottle stopped halfway to his lips, his gaze riveted to a spot just above the slinky black fabric of her bikini bottom. Just to the left of her spine was a heart-shaped birthmark about the size of a fifty cent piece. It was a familiar mark.

A description and photo of just such a mark had been a part of his file at the agency, a means of identifying him, alive or dead. A heart-shaped birthmark just to the left of his spine.

A birthmark exactly like the one Beth had.

She dived into the pool, her body arching over the cool blue water. Jake didn't see the dive. He didn't see anything but that tanned back and that small red mark. A rather insignificant mark really, the kind of thing you hardly noticed and quickly forgot.

He remembered his father telling him once that he had a birthmark just like the one Jake had and that his father had had the same mark. He'd been a little boy at the time and he'd thought it was exciting that he and his father shared something so personal, a visible link between them.

A sort of inheritance passed from father to son.

To daughter.

He was aware that his hand was shaking as he lowered the bottle. He reached out blindly, setting it on a table.

Beth was his daughter.

The simple idea was stunning in its impact. He had a child. Why hadn't he ever made the connection? No one had lied about Beth's age. Was it possible that no one knew?

Feeling eyes on him, he turned his head, his gaze colliding with Josie's. She'd moved down to the pool—to keep an eye on him and Beth?—and now stood a short distance away. Staring at her, he read the truth in her eyes.

She knew. She'd known all along that Frank wasn't Beth's father.

He saw the realization come up in her eyes that the secret she'd kept for twenty years was no longer a secret. Hard on its heels came fear. Jake held her gaze for several long, slow seconds, watching the fear build in her eyes.

He looked away at last, glancing toward the pool where Beth was laughing and splashing with her friends. Out of the corner of his eyes, he saw Josie take a quick step forward as if to thrust herself between him and her daughter. His daughter.

Jake spun on his heel, feeling as dazed as if he'd just received a sharp blow to the head. The lawn full of laughing people looked out of focus, like something seen in a funhouse mirror. A tangle of emotions roiled in him, making him almost sick. Rage. Anguish. Elation. Shock.

Moving quickly through the crowd, he found Paige. She was standing next to Ethel Levine, her expression making it clear that she was only half listening to what the woman was saying. Relief sparked in her eyes when she saw Jake approaching.

"Let's go." He was beyond caring that he was being rude. If Paige thought of protesting, he didn't give her a chance. His hand closed like a manacle around her wrist. He nodded to Ethel, whose eyes were snapping with excitement, her pale blue hair almost quivering with pleasure at this opportunity to witness the way Jake Quincannon treated the woman everyone knew he was having an affair with.

Paige glanced at Jake, startled. But any protest she might have made died when she saw the look on his face. He barely gave her time to say goodbye to Ethel. She knew that Ethel wasn't going to waste any time in telling her cronies that Jake had practically dragged her off, but that couldn't be helped. Obviously, something was very wrong.

Jake led her through the crowd at a pace that raised a few eyebrows. Paige kept a pleasant smile on her face as if nothing was wrong but she was glad her legs were long enough to allow her to keep up with him. She had the feeling that he only half remembered he had hold of her.

She waited until they were almost to the bike before speaking.

"Are you going to tell me what happened or are you just going to drag me all the way home?"

Jake stopped next to the bike, turning a look of such intensity on her that she felt her heart skip a beat.

"Beth went swimming."

"I think half the teenagers in town are in the pool."

"She was wearing this bikini, hardly more than a couple of scraps of fabric." He stopped, staring blindly at her.

"Jake, you didn't drag me out of there because Beth was wearing an indecent swimsuit."

"She has a birthmark on her lower back. It's shaped like a heart. I recognized it." He blinked, his gaze finally focusing on her. "I have one just like it."

Paige sucked in her breath as she realized what he was saying. "Jake..."

"She's mine, Paige. My daughter."

Chapter Twelve

Jake rang the doorbell, listening to the elegant chimes ringing somewhere inside the big house. The columns and wide porch looked even more pretentious than they had the first time he'd seen them. Or maybe it only seemed that way because of the mood he was in.

He'd waited to confront Josie until he was sure Beth would have left for the bank. Beth. His daughter. He still couldn't quite grasp the reality of it. Paige had been nearly as stunned as he was. They'd talked but there hadn't really been much to say.

Beth was his daughter and he'd been cheated out of the chance to know her.

The door opened slowly. Josie stared at him, her expression haunted.

"I think we'd better talk." Jake didn't particularly feel like bothering with the niceties this morning. What he really felt like doing was shaking her until her teeth rattled.

"We don't have anything to talk about." She tried to sound haughty but her voice shook, betraying her nervousness.

"We're going to talk, Josie," Jake said with icy calm. "We can talk here on the doorstep or we can talk inside. I don't really give a damn *where* we talk but we *are* going to talk."

"You really are offensive," she snapped. But she opened the door wider. Jake followed her across the marble-tiled foyer and into the library. Josie shut the double doors behind them, moving nervously into the center of the room.

"What do you want to talk about?"

"Cut the games, Josie." Jake felt almost weary. "Beth is my daughter, isn't she?"

"Don't be ridiculous." But her voice lacked conviction and the look she shot him held more fear than indignation.

"Why didn't you tell me?"

"When?" She set down the figurine she'd been toying with, straightening her shoulders as she turned to face him. "You left, remember?"

"I came back. I told you I was coming back. If you'd written, I could have gotten leave or something and come back even sooner. My God, didn't you think I had a right to know you were carrying my child?"

"You left," she repeated stubbornly. "I didn't know if you'd really come back. When I found out I was pregnant, I was scared."

"So you married Frank? Without even giving me a chance?"

"I married Frank. He was nice and he'd been in love with me all the time you and I were going out together. Besides, you didn't have any plans for the future beyond the service. Frank was on his way to college and then law school."

"So his prospects were better?"

"That's right. I didn't particularly fancy the idea of living in a trailer somewhere and growing old watching you ride your stupid motorcycles. With Frank, I had a chance at a good life. The kind of life I wanted.''

"And what about the baby? Didn't you think I might have wanted to know that I was going to be a father? Didn't you think I'd care? My God, did you even tell Frank it wasn't his?''

"She told me.'' Frank pushed the door the rest of the way open, stepping into the room. Jake turned to look at him. Meeting the other man's eyes, he felt a shock of pain. He hadn't wanted to believe that Frank had known.

It was funny, even after twenty years, he'd always thought of Frank as his best friend, as if the bonds they'd forged when they were young could never be truly broken.

Last night, staring up at the darkened ceiling, listening to Paige's quiet breathing beside him, he'd gone over the events of twenty years ago in his head. He'd almost convinced himself that Frank couldn't have known the truth then, maybe still didn't know the truth.

If he'd known then, he surely couldn't have kept it from Jake, not from his best friend. And if he'd found out later, maybe he'd thought it would cause more trouble than anything else. But he couldn't have known then. Not when Jake had come home from boot camp to find his whole world shattered.

"I'm sorry, Jake.''

"Sorry? Are you apologizing for what happened twenty years ago or are you sorry I found out at all? God, Frank!'' Jake swung away from the man he'd called friend, only to turn back, his expression full of pain. "You were my best friend, the one person I knew I could trust. I came home to find you'd married my girl and now I find out you kept my daughter from me for nineteen years. Why?''

"Because that's the way Josie wanted it." Frank crossed to his wife, touching her lightly on the shoulder as if reassuring her that everything was going to be all right. "I had to respect Josie's wishes, Jake."

"Even at the price of my never knowing I had a child?" Jake questioned, his voice pained.

"If you'd never known, there'd have been no harm done," Frank pointed out.

"I bet you're a hell of a lawyer, Frank." Jake didn't try to hide his contempt. "So you felt it was a victimless crime. Since I didn't know, I couldn't be hurt."

Frank flushed. He ran his hand over his thinning hair. "I guess it does sound like a rather spurious argument, but at the time it seemed like the best thing."

"At the time? What about later? Did it seem as good later?"

"Later it was too late to change anything. We'd already made the decision. You were gone. There didn't seem to be any reason to stir up trouble."

"God forbid we should stir up trouble," Jake said nastily. He stuffed his hands into the pockets of his jeans, afraid that, if he didn't, he was going to break something, preferably someone's neck.

"Does Beth know you're not her father?"

Frank winced at Jake's dismissal of his role in Beth's life, but he didn't protest. It was Josie who jumped in to answer the question.

"She doesn't know and you can't tell her, Jake. She adores Frank. It would break her heart if she found out."

"Found out you'd lied to her all her life, you mean?"

"We didn't lie to her. Frank *is* her father in all the most important ways. He's provided for her far better than you ever could have."

"That's enough, Josie."

Jake's mouth twisted into a bitter smile. "It's a little late to be trying to spare my feelings, Frank."

"Recriminations aren't important now," Frank said quietly. "It's Beth's happiness that's most important now. What do you plan to do, Jake?"

Jake stared at him, the question tumbling around in his head. *What did he plan to do?* Why had he even bothered to come here? Because he wanted to hear Josie confirm what he already knew? He didn't know what he planned to do. He could barely think of anything beyond the fact that he had a fully grown daughter.

"I don't know what I'm going to do," he said at last.

"You can't tell her, Jake," Josie said, her voice rising. "You can't do that to her. She'll never forgive me."

Jake's eyebrow rose. "Never forgive *you*? Do you really think I give a damn about whether or not she forgives you, Josie? You kept my child from me. I'm afraid your feelings aren't a high priority with me at the moment."

"Josie and I are concerned about Beth, Jake. I don't think any of us want to see her hurt."

Frank's reasonableness was harder to deal with than Josie's impending hysteria. Jake wanted to go find Beth and tell her that he was her father. He wanted to go buy a bottle of whiskey and drink himself into oblivion. He wanted to be able to go back twenty years and change everything.

Suddenly the pretentious room with its walls of walnut shelves was suffocating. Without another word, he turned and strode from the room, aware that Josie started after him, only to be stopped by Frank.

It wasn't until he was astride the Harley, the engine's roar in his ears, that he felt as if he could breathe again.

What was he going to do, they'd asked. He didn't have the slightest idea.

"ARE YOU all right?"

Paige set her hands on Jake's shoulders, feeling the knots of tension. He'd been sitting on the back porch, staring out at the mountains which were visible over the fence. He'd been sitting there when she'd come home two hours ago and she didn't think he'd moved since. There was a whiskey bottle and a shot glass beside him but the bottle was still full, the glass empty.

She'd left him alone. There didn't seem to be much she could say, any real comfort she could offer. She couldn't give him back all the years he'd missed with Beth. She couldn't tell him why Josie had chosen to marry Frank rather than tell Jake she was carrying his child.

But he couldn't sit staring at the mountains forever.

"Jake, are you all right?" She had to repeat her question. He stirred as if coming awake, wiping his hand over his face.

"I'm all right."

"Did you see Josie?" Her fingers kneaded his shoulders, trying to work some of the tension out.

"I saw her," he said flatly. "And Frank."

"Frank?" Paige's hands stilled for a moment. "Does he know?"

"He's known from the start. Said it was what Josie wanted." He sounded more weary than bitter and Paige's heart ached for him.

"I'm sorry."

The words were completely inadequate but she couldn't think of anything else to offer. They sat there in silence, watching the last of the light fade from the mountaintops.

"Do you want me to call your parents and tell them we can't make it tonight?"

Jake shifted under her hands and shook his head. "No. It's okay. I'll go clean up."

Paige watched him as he went back into the house and then her eyes turned to the whiskey bottle as if she might find some answers there.

She was no closer to finding those answers an hour later when the Harley stopped in front of the Quincannons' neat house. It had been Jake's mother who had suggested that he bring Paige to dinner, issuing the invitation at the barbecue yesterday, her cool gray eyes studying Paige as if wondering what she might see in Jake.

Paige didn't doubt that the invitation had been issued more out of a sense of duty than real affection. She'd seen the way Jake looked when he came back from one of his infrequent visits with his parents—lost and almost beaten—and she didn't think there was a lot of affection there.

She'd dressed carefully for the visit, sensing that Jake wanted this to go well. The slacks she wore were neatly tailored black linen and she'd topped them with an emerald-green blouse that emphasized the color of her eyes. She'd thrown a jacket on over the outfit, feeling a twinge at the necessity of having to do so.

Summer was officially over with the passing of Labor Day. The nights were cooling off. It wouldn't be that long before frost blackened the marigolds that had been so bright and colorful all summer long.

And Jake would be leaving soon.

She'd forced herself to face that. He hadn't said anything but she could sense a certain restlessness in him, as if he'd been here too long already. She didn't think finding out Beth's true parentage was going to change his mind.

No matter how much he might wish it were different, Frank had been Beth's father all her life. Even if Jake were to tell her the truth—and it would have to come from him if she were ever going to know—nothing could change the fact that he hadn't been the one to stay up nights when she was cutting her first tooth. Or to hold her first bicycle while she found her balance and kiss her bruised knee when she lost it.

All those memories, all those years belonged to Frank.

If anything, finding out that Beth was his daughter seemed more likely to encourage Jake to leave rather than stay.

But sufficient unto the day is the evil thereof, she told herself, running a comb through her hair. Motorcycles were not kind to elaborate hairstyles, so she'd settled on letting it hang straight down her back.

Jake waited while she combed out the tangles, his hands stuffed into his pockets, his shoulders hunched as if carrying too great a weight. The porch light barely reached the end of the path. He was little more than a dark shadow in the dim light.

She dropped the comb into her purse and linked her arm through his. It took an effort to put a smile on her face but she managed it, determined to make the best of the evening.

"Is there anything I should particularly avoid doing besides the usual stuff like eating with my fingers and blowing my nose on the tablecloth?"

Jake blinked and looked down at her as if trying to remember where they were. As they began to walk toward the front door, she could feel the muscles under her hand tense, becoming hard as iron. She wasn't sure how much of the tension was caused by the discovery about Beth and how much by the upcoming meal with his parents.

"You're asking the wrong person," he said at last. "I always seemed able to drive my mother crazy just by breathing."

"I'm afraid that's one thing I can't bring myself to give up."

"She probably won't mind it as much when you do it." He reached up to push the doorbell, his arm tightening, trapping her hand against his side.

His father opened the door.

"Jacob. Paige." He nodded as he pushed open the screen door. "You're a mite late. Mother's fit to be tied."

Mother might be fit to be tied but she was clearly making an effort to hide it. Jake's father led them directly into the dining room. From the way Jake raised his brows, Paige guessed that this was something of an honor. The room was filled to overflowing by a heavy walnut dining-room set. Table, chairs, sideboard, china cabinet and linen chest all crammed into a room that would have been hard-pressed to contain the table alone.

"What a lovely dining room set," Paige said with sincerity.

"It was a wedding gift from my parents. Actually, we rarely use this room."

"I seem to recall being threatened with dismemberment if I so much as set foot in here," Jake commented.

Margaret glanced at her son, her eyes cool in the lamplight. They held none of the affection one would have expected a mother's eyes to show.

"You were a destructive child," she said, as if all children weren't destructive.

It wasn't the last uncomfortable moment of the evening. Paige hadn't been close to her parents but she'd certainly never experienced the thinly veiled hostility that existed in the Quincannon household, particularly between Jake and his mother. His father seemed to serve as a sort of referee and occasional conciliator.

Mother and son disagreed on every subject that came up, from the way to prune and hedge to the meaning of life, or so it seemed to Paige. Jake generally tried to sidestep the issue but Margaret followed like a small dog with a bone, not satisfied until the disagreement had been brought out in the open. As if the fact that he disagreed with her was another piece of proof that he was unworthy.

Paige's appetite deserted her early in the meal. Was this what he'd grown up with? This constant harping on every fault, those coolly critical eyes watching every move he made, ready to pounce on the smallest mistake?

By the time the pie was served, Paige had a knot in her stomach. The flaky crust encompassing a thick layer of apples looked about as appealing as a dead fish but she pinned a smile on her face.

"This looks like a wonderful crust, Mrs. Quincannon. Perhaps you'll give me the recipe?"

She caught the look Jake slanted her and knew that he was thinking about how seldom she cooked anything more complicated than a frozen dinner. She didn't care if she was being obvious. If they started arguing over the pie, she was going to scream.

"Of course, Paige. It was my mother's recipe."

"Mother makes the best pie in the county," Lawrence said heartily. Paige wondered if he was also trying to keep the conversation neutral. It didn't matter. Surely it was possible to have ten minutes of normal conversation. Unfortunately, her next words destroyed any hope of that.

"My niece, Beth, thinks apple pie is one of the four food groups."

She'd been so desperate to keep the innocuous conversation going that she was halfway through the sentence before she realized what she'd said. Bringing up Beth had not been the most intelligent thing to do. She glanced at Jake, worried that she'd reminded him of something he'd probably like to forget, at least for a little while.

But Jake wasn't looking at her. His gaze was on his mother and the intensity of that look was enough to burn holes through wood. Glancing at her hostess, Paige saw that she was looking at her plate. This in itself was nothing unusual except that the knuckles of her fingers were white from the force with which she gripped her fork.

"You knew," Jake said hoarsely.

Paige's heart bumped as she realized what he was saying. He thought his parents knew that Beth was his child, their grandchild. It wasn't possible. But the guilt in his father's eyes gave her the answer even as she asked the question.

"Look at me, Mother."

The eyes she lifted to his face were as cool and unemotional as ever. But Jake didn't seem to have any trouble reading the truth there.

"How long have you known she was my daughter?"

"Now, Jacob, there's no call to go getting in a fuss about it. It's all long over and done with." But the waters that had been whipped up across the snowy tablecloth were much too turbulent for Lawrence's rather feeble effort at calming them down.

"My God, how long have you known? Answer me, dammit!"

"There's no call for profanity, Jacob." Margaret set her fork beside her untouched plate, arranging it with neat precision. "Your father and I have known almost from the beginning that Beth was our grandchild."

The fact that he'd already guessed the truth didn't cushion the impact of her words. He'd known all his life that his mother didn't feel about him the way mothers usually felt about their children. When he was small, he'd tried desperately to gain her approval. Failing that, he'd settled for any reaction he could pull from her, usually anger.

But he'd never have believed she'd keep something like this from him. If not for his sake, then for hers. Hadn't she wanted a chance to get to know her grandchild? He didn't realize he'd asked the question out loud until she answered him.

"Frank always made it a point to bring Beth by occasionally. We were able to watch her grow up."

"Why didn't you ever tell me?"

"It seemed best not to," his mother said in her quiet way. His father stared at the tablecloth.

"Why? Why did it seem best to keep my child from me?" Jake's hand clenched into a fist on the table. Somewhere inside he could feel rage and pain boiling, threatening to spill over and destroy his control.

"We felt Frank could do more for our grandchild than you ever could. With all your traveling all over the world, doing God knows what. Killing and destroying, no doubt. What could you possibly have offered a sweet little girl?"

The words were all the more cruel for having been delivered in that cool, unemotional tone. Jake felt the color draining from his face. Staring at his mother, he felt true hatred for the first time in his life.

He hated her for all the years he'd spent trying to make her love him and never understanding why she didn't. He hated her for sitting there looking as if they were discussing whether to have tea or coffee. And he hated her for keeping Beth from him.

Josie and Frank had made their choices in a tangle of emotions. Maybe they'd really believed they were doing the right thing. But he knew, beyond a shadow of a doubt, that his mother had kept the secret for twenty years, not out of concern for Beth, but because she enjoyed the knowledge of how much it would hurt him if he ever found out.

"That was uncalled for, Margaret." His father's voice held a stern note he'd never heard directed toward his mother, but the words couldn't be taken back, even if she'd wanted to. And she didn't want to.

Without another word, Jake shoved back his chair, barely noticing when it slammed against the china cabinet. He strode from the room, knowing that he had to get fresh air. Knowing that, if he stayed, he couldn't guarantee he wasn't going to hit his own mother.

The silence he left behind was deafening. Paige broke it by pushing back her chair. She paused long enough to fix Margaret Quincannon with a look of contempt that brought a flush to the older woman's face.

"You don't deserve to have a son like Jake. Someday you're going to be a lonely old woman because people like you always end up like that. And I hope to God you remember what you've done and have to live with regret to your last bitter breath."

She tossed her napkin on the table and strode from the room without another word. Snatching her jacket off the coat rack, she hurried out the front door. Jake was already astride the Harley, gunning the big engine to life as Paige ran down the path. She skidded to a halt next to him.

"You're better off walking home," he said without looking at her, his voice carrying easily over the roar of the engine. "Or call Martin and ask him to give you a ride."

"Where are you going?"

"I don't know."

"I'm coming with you."

"I don't want company," he said bluntly.

"Tough."

He looked as if he might carry the argument further but she was already hopping onto the back of the motorcycle. She'd barely settled in place when the big bike took off, the rear wheel spitting gravel as it fought for purchase.

Paige grabbed for his waist, winding her arms around him, burying her face against his back as they roared into the night.

Forever after, she could remember only pieces of that wild ride. Paige clung to him, leaning her body with his when they took corners so fast the bike seemed to lie on the ground. Jake drove as if a demon was riding his shoulder. Which she supposed it was.

When he turned onto the road that led up Borden Hill, she could only close her eyes tighter and offer up an incoherent prayer. He skidded around the iron gates, skirting the edge so close that Paige felt her right foot hanging over empty space.

Taking the last curve too fast, the rear wheel skidded in the loose dirt. Paige gasped as Jake fought to regain control, finally steadying the big bike more by brute strength than anything else.

They came to a halt on the packed dirt of the parking lot. For several seconds, Paige didn't move, not even to lift her head from Jake's shoulder.

"Are you all right?" Jake's voice rumbled beneath her ear. She lifted her head slowly, taking a deep breath before answering him.

"I'm all right."

"I warned you not to come with me." He reached back one hand to help her slide off the bike, waiting until she was on the ground before nudging the kickstand into place and dismounting.

"So you did," Paige agreed, brushing futilely at her tangled hair. "But you should know by now that I rarely do what I should."

He shoved his hands into his pockets, half turning away from her. She could feel his pain as acutely as if it were her own.

"You know she's wrong, Jake. You have to know it."

"Do I?" He stared out over the dark valley.

"You would have been a good father."

"Maybe she's right." He didn't seem to hear her. "Maybe Beth was better off without me."

"That's not true." Since he wouldn't look at her, she moved to stand in front of him, taking hold of his arm, demanding that he listen. "You're a good man, Jake. No matter how hard you try to pretend you're not, you are. Beth would have been lucky to grow up with you as her father. Your parents were wrong not to tell you about her."

"I used to try so hard to make her love me," Jake said, speaking as much to himself as to her. "Mothers are supposed to love their children. I always knew that and I couldn't understand why she didn't love me. I had a brother, you know."

"I know." Paige stroked his arm.

"He was three years younger than I was. Michael. He died when I was eight. He was everything I wasn't. Blond and sweet. She always said that he had the prettiest blue eyes she'd ever seen. I used to stand in front of the mirror and wonder why my blue eyes weren't pretty, too. Sometimes, I'd think that she'd love me if Michael were gone."

He seemed caught in the grip of memories she couldn't share. Paige wanted to ask what had happened to his brother but she couldn't get the words out past the ache in her throat. He answered the question as if she'd spoken.

"He drowned. It was winter and the river was iced over. She'd told us not to go out on the ice. We were playing and I was supposed to be watching him. Michael went out on the ice and it broke under him. I crawled out after him and managed to grab hold of his hands but he was too heavy and I couldn't pull him up.

"I kept telling him it was going to be all right, that Mama would come help us. 'Mama will come,' I kept saying, over and over again, but by the time she came, it was too late."

Paige could hardly see him through the tears that blinded her. In her mind's eye, she could see the two frightened children, Jake trying to comfort his little brother, trying to push his own fears back.

"It was a tragedy, Jake, but it wasn't your fault."

"I know. I even think I knew it then. But I *had* wondered if she'd love me if he were gone. That was almost like wishing him dead. She never said it was my fault that he died. But sometimes when she'd look at me, I knew she was wishing *I'd* been the one to fall through the ice."

"No. I'm sure she never would have thought that." Her own uncertainty made her denial even more forceful. Perhaps Jake heard the doubt because his mouth twisted as he looked down at her, his expression shadowed in the moonlight.

"She didn't tell me about Beth because she thought I'd be bad for my own child. Maybe she was right."

"No, she wasn't." But he didn't seem to hear her fierce denial.

"I've killed people, Paige. She was right about that. I have spent most of my life killing and destroying. It's all I really know how to do."

The pain in his voice was so profound it left her momentarily speechless. She stared up at him, groping for something to say.

"I love you, Jake." She felt him jerk as if the words had the impact of a bullet. She tightened her hand on his arm. "I love you and since I've always had impeccable taste, you can't be nearly as bad as you think."

"Don't." The word felt thick on his tongue. He looked down at her. The moonlight bleached the color from her skin and hair, giving her the look of a pale wraith. But there was nothing wraithlike in the strength of her fingers on his arm. Nothing ethereal in the steady gaze of those wide green eyes.

She'd just laid her soul bare for him, offered it as a bandage for his pain. No one in his life had ever made themselves so completely vulnerable. That she'd done it to comfort him only made it more threatening.

"God, Paige." He felt something breaking apart inside him, something tight and hard that had been lodged like a rock in his chest. "God."

He caught her to him with bruising strength, burying his face in the tangled length of her hair, holding her as if he couldn't bear to let her go.

Chapter Thirteen

Paige was gone when Jake awoke the next morning. He missed the feel of her in his arms but he was somewhat relieved. He wasn't sure he was ready to face her yet. Last night she'd soothed his pain, even though it meant opening herself up to hurt.

She'd said she loved him.

He rolled the idea over in his mind, feeling it flow over him like cool water over fevered skin.

He'd have to leave. He scowled at the ceiling. No matter what she said, he knew, better than she ever could, that he was no good for anything more than a summer affair. She didn't understand what he'd been, the scars he carried, the nightmares that sometimes woke him up screaming things he couldn't even remember as the sound died.

No, he was carrying too much emotional baggage. He couldn't burden her with it. She'd never believe him if he told her that now. But maybe someday she'd understand.

He'd leave today. Other than Paige there was no one to keep him in this town. No one who'd care if he left and more than a few who'd be relieved. Summer was over. It was time to move on.

But he made no move to start packing. Telling himself that he wanted to say goodbye to Pop, he dressed and drove the Harley into town, parking behind the bank.

There seemed to be more people in town than usual. Jake wondered if he was imagining the faint autumnal bustle in the air. The sun was shining brightly but it didn't feel as warm on his shoulders as it had a week ago, as if some of the strength had gone out of it.

"Jake!" Pop's creased features lit up in a pleased smile as Jake pushed open the bank door. The air conditioning that had seemed pleasantly cool a few days ago now seemed chilly.

"Catch any bank robbers yet?" Jake asked as Pop got to his feet.

"Not yet, but I'm ready." The old man patted the holstered gun at his side, his grin emphasizing the joke. "Saw you at the barbecue the other day. You took out of there pretty fast."

Jake's smile faded. "I suppose I did." He glanced toward the back of the bank. "Beth Hudson working today?"

"Yup. Went to lunch about twenty minutes ago. Cute little thing."

"Yeah, she is." It was probably just as well that she was gone, Jake told himself. The fact that they shared blood didn't change anything. And he'd always hated saying goodbye.

He lingered with Pop a few minutes longer, talking about nothing in particular. He was delaying the moment when he'd have to say that he was leaving. Once he said it, it would be real, irrevocable. He could just leave without saying anything but he owed Pop more than that.

"Pop, I—"

"Mr. Bellows, I don't see how you can properly guard my bank when you spend all your time talking to your friends." Henry Nathan, president of Riverbend's only bank, puffed across the floor, his hushed voice preceding him.

Pop frowned, rolling his eyes at Jake before turning to his employer. "Sorry, Mr. Nathan. Seeing as how there wasn't anyone in here but you and Lisa Mae at the window—no customers and all—I figured there wasn't a whole lot to worry about."

"I pay you to be on guard duty at all times, Mr. Bellows, not when you think it's convenient. The payroll is due in this afternoon and it might help if you at least pretended to show an interest in its safe delivery."

Jake wondered if Nathan would look any better with his nose broken in two or three places. But it wasn't his place to interfere in his friend's business. To do so would only be an embarrassment to Pop.

"I was just leaving." He pushed himself away from the pillar he'd been leaning against, deliberately looming over Nathan, who took a quick step back. Jake gave him a slow smile, enjoying the uneasy look that came into the man's eyes.

"I'll be seeing you later, Jake."

"Sure. I'll stop by later, Pop." He could stop by on his way out of town and say goodbye.

He stepped out into the street, narrowing his eyes against the sun. He still had to tell Paige he was going. God alone knew how he was going to do that.

PAIGE GLANCED UP as the library door opened, her expression chilling when she saw who had entered.

Josie caught her sister's eyes and seemed to hesitate a moment before advancing boldly.

Paige was vaguely surprised by the strength of the rage she felt. She'd never particularly liked her sister but her feelings for her now ran close to hatred. She'd never imagined she was capable of such an emotion.

"Have you come to check out a book, Josie?"

Josie flushed at Paige's tone but she didn't stop until she stood just across the desk. Paige stood up slowly, her eyes meeting Josie's straight on.

"I want to talk to you," Josie said.

"Really? I can't imagine what about."

"Have you . . . talked to Jake?"

"If what you're asking is do I know that Beth is his daughter, the answer is yes."

"Quiet!" Josie's eyes darted around to see if anyone could have overheard Paige.

"There's only the two of us here, Josie."

"Well, you can never be too careful."

"You would know. You've built your life so carefully, haven't you? Never giving a damn about who you use in the process. Mom and Dad, me, Jake, Frank. Is there anyone you really care about?"

"I can see you're going to take Jake's side in this," Josie said, her tone hurt. "I only did what I thought was best for my baby. Even all those years ago it was plain to see that Frank could give us more security than Jake could.

"And I was obviously right. Look at the way he's come back here with nothing to show for the last twenty years but that awful motorcycle.

"Besides, it's not as if keeping Beth's parentage a secret caused Jake any harm. He's a little upset now but he'll see that I did the best thing."

Paige clenched her hands into fists as she struggled against the urge to smack Josie until her ears rang. To hear her dismiss Jake's anguish as "a little upset" made her blood drum in her ears.

"What do you want, Josie?"

Josie looked a little surprised by the flat question but she seized her opportunity. "I know you want what's best for Beth, Paige. After all, she's completely innocent in this. No one wants to see her hurt."

"Cut to the chase. What do you want?"

"I want you to talk Jake out of telling her that...that..."

"That he's her father?" Paige finished, arching one eyebrow.

"Yes. The truth isn't going to do anything but hurt her now."

"So you want me to convince Jake to walk out of her life right after he's discovered that he's her father."

"Well, it isn't as if he *knows* her or anything. I mean, they're really hardly more than strangers. Besides, you owe me this much, Paige."

"I *owe* you?" Paige asked, astonished to discover that Josie could still surprise her.

"If it hadn't been for you, he would have left town weeks ago," Josie said with a touch of indignation. "No one would have ever had to know about this."

"And that would make all the lies okay?"

"Don't sound so self-righteous," Josie snapped, suddenly dropping the pretense of maternal concern. "You fell into bed with him like a cheap tramp. Or a starved spinster," she added spitefully.

"A starved spinster?" Paige stared at her for a moment and then laughed, a sound of such genuine amusement that Josie's face flushed an ugly shade of red.

Paige was still smiling when the big door banged open, slamming against the wall behind it in a way guaranteed to put gouges in the paneling. Mary tumbled through the door, breathless, as if she'd been running. Urgency seemed to spill into the room with her.

"What's wrong?" Paige asked, coming around the desk, her heart thumping with fear. What if something had happened to Jake?

"There's been a robbery at the bank," Mary got out between gulps of air. "They've taken hostages."

"My God. Beth." Josie pressed her hand to the base of her throat. Glancing at her sister's pale face, Paige was surprised to realize that Josie really did love her daughter. "I've got to get over there."

She brushed past Mary, her heels clicking on the wooden floor as she ran out. Paige would have followed her but she suddenly thought to tell Jake. She punched out the phone number, her fingers shaking so badly that she had to redial. The phone rang and rang but no one answered. She slammed the receiver down, turning to Mary.

"Have you seen Jake?"

"He was with Martin earlier. I saw them talking."

If he was still with Martin, then he would already know what had happened.

JAKE WAS INDEED with Martin. They'd been standing beside Martin's patrol car when the call came in. On the heels of the alarm had come the sound of shots fired from the bank. Jake had spun into a crouch, reaching for the gun he no longer carried, every sense instantly alert.

That had been nearly thirty minutes ago. Since then, there hadn't been a sound from the bank. Martin had moved quickly, blocking off the street in front of the bank, clearing people out of the area.

He'd set up a temporary headquarters in the building across the street from the bank, which just happened to be the post office. No one had said a word when Jake joined the small gathering. The office offered a clear view of the bank. Too clear, Jake thought bleakly.

Pop Bellows lay sprawled just inside the doors, the gun he'd patted laughingly a couple of hours ago only half drawn. That he was dead was something Jake didn't doubt. He'd seen enough bodies to recognize the sprawl of limbs, the look of death.

Somewhere deep inside, Jake felt a terrible grief but there was no time to give in to it now. The man had been more of a father to him than a friend. He'd believed in the young Jake when no one else did. Jake turned away, forcing his grief down. Pop was dead but he'd died in the way he would have wished to, trying to help someone.

But somewhere inside the bank was Beth, alive and unhurt, he hoped. Beth and the other teller. Nathan had escaped out the window of his office when he heard the alarm go off and he'd told Martin that he didn't think there were any customers in the bank. Just the two women.

Looking at his pasty, sweaty face, Jake told himself that it was unfair to blame Nathan for escaping. There was nothing he could have done against two gunmen who were clearly prepared to shoot to kill.

But he kept thinking of how frightened Beth must be.

"They were crazy, Sheriff Smith." Nathan wiped one fat-fingered hand over his sweaty forehead. "On drugs or something. I saw what happened through my office door. They shot Pop Bellows as quick as stepping on a cockroach and then laughed about it."

He clutched the glass of water someone had handed him, his hand shaking so badly the water threatened to slosh over the rim. "There wasn't anything I could do. Lisa Mae must have stepped on the alarm button. I saw the light go on and then I climbed out the window."

Though Jake thought his face was expressionless, Nathan flushed when he glanced at him. "There wasn't anything I could do," he repeated defensively, though Jake hadn't said a word.

"No one said there was, Mr. Nathan." Martin's voice was calm, in control. There was a commotion at the back door, one of the deputies arguing with someone, and then Josie rushed into the room. Frank was behind her and behind him was Paige.

Jake's gaze met hers across the room. It was like falling into a cool green stream. He read comfort and sympathy in her eyes. He didn't have to ask if she knew about Pop. He could see that she did and that she understood his grief. That she knew about Beth being inside the bank was obvious when Josie began to speak, demanding that Martin do something.

Frank set his hands on her shoulders, leaning down to murmur something in her ear. For a moment, it seemed as if she was going to ignore him and then she seemed to crumple, turning to him and burying her face against his shoulder.

Frank glanced at Jake over her head and then looked at Martin. "What's the situation, Sheriff? Is Beth all right?"

"We don't really know much at the moment, Frank, and that's the honest truth. As far as we know, Beth and Lisa Mae are fine. But I'm not going to lie to you. There's two men in there with guns and they've already killed Pop Bellows. We got them on the phone a little while ago but they said they'd call us when they wanted to talk and not to call back or they'd kill one of the girls."

Frank's face had grown more pale and stern as Martin talked. Josie began to sob, her fingers digging into the front of her husband's jacket. Looking at Paige, Jake saw her bite her lip, the fear apparent in her eyes.

He wanted to go to her, hold her and tell her that it was going to be all right. But he was too full of fear himself to offer reassurance to anyone else. He turned back to the window, staring at the bank, trying not to think about Pop's motionless body. Behind him, he could hear Martin's quiet voice.

Pop had done a good job with him, Jake thought. Martin was one hell of a lawman. He'd responded to the emergency as if he did this every day in some big city precinct. Pop would have been proud.

"What do you think?" Martin had moved up to stand next to Jake, his eyes reflecting his own grief when he looked across the street at Pop's body.

"I think we've got a nasty situation here." Neither man noticed the use of the plural. "If Nathan is right and these guys are on something..." Jake let his voice trail off, shrugging. "There's no telling what they might do."

"If we go in with guns blazing, one or both of the girls could end up hurt or dead," Martin said, thinking out loud. "I say we wait for them to call."

"That's what I'd suggest, too. They can't stay in there forever. Sooner or later, they're going to have to try and bargain their way out of this."

When the phone rang fifteen minutes later, everyone jumped. Martin let the phone ring once, twice before picking it up. The silence in the crowded room could have been cut with a knife as everyone leaned forward, their attention focused on Martin.

He listened, speaking mostly in monosyllables at first. It wasn't hard to guess that the robbers were making their demands.

"You're asking for a lot," Martin said, his tone calm and reasonable. "It's going to take some time to arrange all this. No, I'm not trying to stall. I'm just going to need some time, that's all.

"If I'm going to arrange this for you, I'd like a little something from you. I need some proof that the hostages are all right."

His jaw tightened but his voice didn't change. "No. I have to have proof that they're alive and unhurt."

The sound of a gunshot echoed clearly from across the street. Jake jerked as if the sound had hit him with the impact of a bullet. Josie screamed and went limp in Frank's arm. Paige stumbled back against the wall behind her, her eyes enormous in her pale face.

"Dammit! There was no reason to do that." Martin's voice had lost some of its calm reason. Jake saw his jaw knotting with the effort of staving off panic. "All right. You've made your point. One hour."

He set the receiver down and spoke without looking up. "He says they've wounded one of the hostages. He says next time he'll shoot to kill."

"Maybe he just fired into the air," Paige said, her face so pale Jake wondered if she was going to faint, too. "Just to frighten us."

"What do they want?" Jake asked quietly.

"A helicopter in front of the bank and a plane waiting for them at the nearest airport. The one I spoke to says he's a pilot. He claims they'll let the girls go as soon as they get to Mexico."

"You don't believe him?" That was Paige, who'd come up to stand next to Jake.

Martin shook his head slowly. "The guy doesn't sound rational, Paige. I'm sorry. As soon as they don't need them for protection..." Martin didn't have to complete his thought. Everyone in the tight, suddenly airless room knew his meaning.

Paige nodded, her teeth worrying her lip. "What are you going to do?"

Martin ran his hand through his ruddy hair. "I'm going to arrange for a helicopter. We can't do anything about them as long as they're inside, and they won't come out until they see a chopper."

"But you already said that you think they'll kill the girls." That was Frank. He'd laid Josie on a low sofa where she was just starting to stir.

"We've got to get them out of the bank before we can do anything, Frank. Once they're out, I think we have to try and pick them off."

"Pick them off? My God, you mean, shoot them?" Frank sounded horrified. "They're sure to bring the girls with them."

"I know. But it will be our best chance. Two snipers with rifles would have a good line of fire from the roof of this building. I think it's the best chance we have."

Frank looked as though he might have wanted to say more but Josie called his name and he turned back to her. She was weeping quietly, her makeup running down her pale cheeks. Gone was the sophisticated, self-centered woman; in her place was a mother terrified for the safety of her child. Paige almost forgave her for hurting Jake. Almost.

"It's going to take some careful shooting," Jake said. "You're only going to have one chance and if you miss..." He finished the sentence with a slight shrug.

"I've got a man who could shoot a dime off a fence post at fifty feet and never touch wood. He'll hit anything he aims at."

"You're going to need two men." That was Frank.

"I know." Martin looked at Jake.

Paige bit back a protest. Not Jake. Martin couldn't ask Jake to do this. He already carried a heavy load of guilt for the killing he'd done in his past. And this was Beth. Martin didn't know what he was asking Jake to do. If something went wrong, Jake would never be able to live with it.

Jake's stomach knotted as he looked at Martin. All eyes had turned to him, a mixture of hope and fear in them. He'd known what was going to happen. They all knew he had the skill required to hit a gunman without harming a hostage. They all guessed he'd done similar jobs in the past.

He turned away from those hopeful eyes, staring out the window. He'd sworn to himself that he was through with all of that. No more dark alleys, no more walking in the shadows, no more guns. No more killing.

Was he really through with it? Maybe you couldn't ever walk away from something like that. Maybe it followed you forever, haunting you, a part of you whether you wanted it to be or not.

He couldn't do it.

But this was for Beth. For her life. The daughter he hadn't even known he had.

And if he missed? If he missed and one of them killed her? Or God forbid, what if his own bullet . . . ?

No. He wouldn't think about that.

He didn't really have a choice. He stared down at his hands. He was the best chance Beth had. He had, unknowingly, given her life twenty years ago. He had to try and preserve that life now.

"All right." He turned back to Martin. "You've got your second sniper."

THERE WAS A TOUCH of bitter irony, he thought thirty minutes later, in the way everyone's attitude suddenly changed when his dangerous skills came in handy. There was nothing Martin could do about the crowd that had gathered behind the post office.

It hadn't taken long for the news of the robbery attempt to spread. Everyone knew there were hostages. Most of these people had known Beth and Lisa Mae all their lives. There was the usual amount of gawking that any dramatic event was bound to draw. But there was also a more personal concern. This was their town, the people involved were known to most of the crowd personally.

There was a murmur as Jake stepped out of the back door of the post office. Jake ignored them as he followed Martin out to the patrol car to select a rifle. The barriers Martin had set up kept the crowd at a distance but he could feel their avid interest as he checked the balance of each weapon, sighting along it, looking for some indefinable feel that made the weapon fit his hand.

The news that they were going to try to pick off the robbers as they came out of the bank spread through the crowd like wildfire. Everyone knew Slim Johnson and no one was surprised to see him there. But seeing Jake Quincannon there was a bit of a shock. Those who had seen his shooting at the fair whispered knowingly to those who hadn't been there. People who had eyed him uneasily the day before were suddenly looking at him with hope.

Jake blocked the crowd from his mind, concentrating on what Martin was saying. He'd already been introduced to Slim Johnson, a tall lanky man who looked barely out of his teens, though Jake would have put his age at closer to twenty-five. The rifle Slim carried was well worn and he held it as if it were a part of his body. Jake didn't doubt the man could hit anything he aimed at. The question was, had he ever had to shoot another man before?

"The chopper should be here in ten or fifteen minutes," Martin was saying. "I've told the pilot to set it down slightly to the south of the bank. That should give you a clear field of fire. If you can't get a clear shot, don't try anything. I've alerted the airport in Seattle, where the plane is waiting for them. If we can't end this here, we'll let the Seattle police handle it."

"We'll handle it," Slim said calmly.

"I hope so. Good luck." Martin's handshake was firm, his eyes direct. He knew what he was asking. Jake knew if there'd been another way to do it, Martin would have taken it.

Neither he nor Slim spoke as they climbed to the rooftop. Jake dropped to his belly when they reached the roof. Pulling himself along on his elbows, he crept toward the low parapet on the front of the building. Over the edge he had a clear field of fire that encompassed the entire front of the bank.

"When they come out, I'll take whoever is on the left," Jake murmured as Slim crept up beside him.

"Fine by me."

And that was the only conversation they exchanged.

Jake wiped the sweat from his forehead. Was it only today that he'd been thinking that the sun seemed to have lost its summer strength? Lying up here, waiting, it certainly seemed powerful enough.

It reminded him of other times, other places. Saigon, where the heat and humidity had sometimes seemed borne straight from hell. Beirut, which surely had been hell.

He reached up to adjust the eye patch. He couldn't miss. This time, of all times, he couldn't afford to miss. If his whole life had been leading up to this one point, then he had to make sure he didn't fail. Beth's life depended on his success.

Don't think about that. Think about something else.

Like the way Paige's eyes always seemed to smile before her mouth did. Or the way her skin heated beneath his hands. The way she teased him when she thought he was taking himself too seriously.

The fact that he had to leave her.

No. Don't think about that, either.

Don't think about anything beyond the moment. Don't allow a second's doubt to creep in. It wasn't a man he'd be shooting at. It was a target, a silhouette on a shooting range. Not a human being.

He rested his forehead on his arm, staring at the rough surface of the roof. This was just another job. The last he'd ever do.

The most important he'd ever had.

IT SEEMED AS IF hours went by, though in reality it was only a few minutes before he heard the helicopter in the distance. Jake wiped his hands on his jeans, making sure they were perfectly dry before taking hold of the rifle stock and laying it along his cheek.

The wind from the chopper's rotors whipped through his hair as the machine hovered overhead for a moment before slowly setting down in the street. A good pilot, he noted with one part of his mind. He'd set the chopper just south of the bank, far enough to allow a clear field of fire but not far enough to make the men inside too anxious.

There was movement inside the bank and Jake curled his finger around the trigger. The stock rested solidly against his shoulder, the wood warm to the touch. The weapon was an extension of his body, just as it had always been. Looking through the scope, he took a deep breath, deliberately slowing his pulse, aware of each separate beat of his heart.

There was a flurry of movement inside and then the doors were shoved open and the robbers came out, each holding a hostage, using her body as a shield.

Jake focused only on the one to the left. The other one was Slim's problem.

Beth. A muscle ticked in his jaw. His target was the one holding Beth. Her blouse, which must have been crisp and white this morning was torn and soaked with blood down one sleeve and side. Her face was white, her eyes wide and terrified.

Through the scope, he could see the man holding her, all ratty black hair and wild eyes. He was holding an automatic beside Beth's head but not pointed at her. That was good. Less chance of a convulsive finger movement pulling the trigger.

Jake forced Beth's face, her expression of shocked fear from his mind. He only had to think of one thing now. Just one thing.

To PAIGE, the minutes since Jake had gone up to the rooftop seemed to tick by in slow motion. Martin had insisted that everyone wait in back of the post office, protecting them as much from what might happen in front of the bank as he was from stray bullets.

Josie and Frank were sitting in the back of a patrol car. Josie wept loudly, making Paige want to smack her and tell her to shut up. Frank was pale and stern-looking. Paige sat in the front seat, her thoughts torn between fear for Beth and concern for Jake.

She knew, better than anyone, what this could do to him. He'd never told her the details of what his job had been but she didn't need to know the details. She could guess quite a bit.

Whatever Jake had been, she loved him. He'd walked away from that part of his life, put it behind him. Now he was going to have to kill again, this time to save Beth's life.

She supposed that a more charitable woman might have felt some twinge of regret at the thought of the men inside the bank losing their lives. But she wasn't feeling very charitable. They'd killed Pop Bellows. They'd wounded one of the hostages—maybe Beth. They'd made their choices.

She sucked in her breath when she heard the helicopter. Unable to sit still a moment longer, she thrust open the car door and stepped out, shielding her eyes as she watched the helicopter go by so low the pilot was clearly visible. It hovered over the building for a moment before disappearing, as the pilot lowered it into the street.

Paige waited, hardly breathing. She wasn't aware of Frank and Josie getting out of the patrol car to stand beside her. Nor was she aware of the crowd of neighbors and friends who watched from behind the rope barrier.

The shots were so close together they sounded as though they were one—a heavy boom followed by a stunning silence.

Josie screamed, her knuckles turning white where she clutched Frank's sleeve. Paige didn't move. She forgot to breathe. A thousand incoherent prayers tumbled together in her mind.

Martin had been inside the building, watching what was happening on the street. The moments oozed by so slowly they seemed caught in a trap that was sucking them backward. Paige counted. One, two... By the time she got to fifty, he'd bring Beth out, alive and unhurt. Fifty-two, Fifty-three... By the time she reached one hundred, they'd know that everything was all right.

Her head jerked upward as Jake swung over the roof, feeling for the first rung of the ladder. The rifle was slung over his back. There was a murmur as the crowd saw him. Paige started toward him, hesitating as the back door of the post office was thrust open.

"Beth!" That was Josie, her strength suddenly returning. She tore herself away from Frank and rushed to her daughter, who was being half supported, half carried by Martin.

Paige felt tears start to her eyes. She'd noticed, as Josie hadn't yet, the blood on Beth's arm, but she was walking. She was safe.

Jake's feet had just touched ground when he felt Paige behind him. He knew it was her, even before he turned. For a moment, he stayed where he was, staring at the brick wall in front of him.

He'd just killed a man. Was he going to see horror in her eyes? A look that questioned how he could have done such a thing, even to save a life? He'd seen that look before. He didn't think he could bear to see it in Paige's eyes.

"Jake?" Her hand touched his sleeve and he turned, bracing himself for whatever he might see.

"Are you all right?"

The question took his breath away. He'd been forced to kill before and he'd answered all the questions he was thrown afterward by his superiors and the battery of psychiatrists ever ready to jump on any sign that he wasn't properly aware that he'd taken a human life. No one had ever thought to ask him the simple question Paige had just asked.

Was he all right?

God, no. He'd just killed a man. A man who'd murdered Pop and would have killed Beth without hesitation, but another human being nevertheless. He felt filthy, as if he'd just rolled in a sewer. He felt weary, burned-out, used up. No, he wasn't all right.

But looking into Paige's eyes, seeing the concern, the love she didn't try to hide, all those disturbing feelings started to fade.

"I'm okay," he said huskily.

"Thank God." The tears she'd refused to shed earlier began to fall but it didn't matter. She had her arms around Jake, her face pressed against his chest. He hesitated, hardly daring to believe in the reality of her love and then his arms came around her, crushing her closer still. He buried his face in her hair, letting the soft scent of her drive away the memories.

They stood that way for a few moments, oblivious of everything going on around them. Well-wishers crowded around Beth as if they needed to see her up close to believe that she was all right. The other teller was unharmed and sobbing in her husband's arms.

Jake and Paige stood off to the side. When he lifted his head, he wasn't surprised to see the small pool of distance that surrounded them. It wasn't that people weren't glad that he'd been here, that his skills had come in useful. But now that the crisis was over, they were uneasy.

It would have been different if he'd been wearing a uniform. That formalized things somehow, made the killing more respectable. That was just the reason he'd quit. It had begun to seem all right to him, too. And he didn't need a psychiatrist to tell him that when killing no longer left a hollow ache in the pit of your stomach, it was time to get out of the business.

Looking over Paige's head, he saw Beth. Other than the wound in her arm, which didn't look serious from what he could see, she looked all right. It might take her a while to come to terms with what she'd experienced but she was young and she had a good share of common sense. She'd be fine.

Frank had his arms around her shoulders and she was leaning against him like a tired child. The image burned into Jake's mind, settling into a deep ache in his chest. Beth was his daughter by blood but she'd never be his in any real sense. Frank was the father of her heart. Nothing would change that.

He'd lost her without ever really having had her.

Jake's eyes met Frank's for a long moment before he looked away. He bent over Paige.

"Let's go home."

Chapter Fourteen

It was, Paige thought, incredible how quickly life got back to normal. It had been only a week since the attempted robbery, yet everything seemed to be going on as if nothing at all had happened.

She went to work every day. School would be starting in less than a week, which meant the library would be open longer hours. There would be a steady stream of youngsters studying the American Revolution, tree frogs and Watergate.

She usually enjoyed this time of year. Mixed with the regret for summer's passing was a certain excitement at the changing seasons. She loved to see the first ragged vee of geese flying overhead, going south for the winter. But this year, when she saw them, all she could think was that she wished she were going with them.

Pop Bellows was buried two days after the shooting, laid to rest in the cemetery that held graves dating back to the days when the stagecoach had come through once a month, bringing news and supplies to the valley. Paige had stood beside Jake, worried about the total lack of emotion in his face. But when she'd slipped her hand into his, his fingers had closed convulsively over hers.

He'd had a terrible nightmare that night, muttering in his sleep, his face tortured in the moonlight. He woke himself before Paige could. Instinct made her lie still with her eyes shut as if she were still asleep. She'd felt him studying her before he slipped from the bed. Through slitted eyes, she watched him walk to the window, staring out into the darkness as if seeking answers there. He'd stayed there for a long time before finally coming back to bed.

Paige's teeth worried at her lower lip as she stared at the library cards she was supposed to be updating. He was pulling away from her. It was a subtle withdrawal but she knew she wasn't imagining it.

She knew he'd be leaving soon. Summer was over. Whatever he'd hoped to find here was either found or it didn't exist. He'd leave and life would go on but it couldn't ever be the same.

She'd thought that she could say goodbye to him and go on with her life. Oh, it would hurt but she'd known from the beginning that this was only a summer romance. He'd never lied to her about it and she'd accepted their relationship on those terms.

She'd felt it would be enough to have him for a few short months. Her life had needed shaking up. She'd allowed herself to get stuck in a rut, a safe, cozy one but still a rut. Jake had been just what she'd needed to blow her out of that rut.

She hadn't planned on falling in love with him. But even when she realized she was in love with him, she'd told herself that she could watch him walk away. It was going to hurt—more than anything she'd ever known. But it was worth it.

But was her life worth much without him?

She flicked her finger against the stack of cards, fanning them out on the desk. Jake wasn't just going to leave a hole, he was going to leave a gaping tear.

She'd go with him in a minute if he'd ask her. But he'd never ask. Not even if his heart was breaking as much as hers. He was pulling away now but whom was he trying to protect? Her? Or himself?

JAKE SLID THE LAST of his clothes into the shallow duffel and zipped it shut. He was taking only what he'd brought with him. Though in truth he was leaving a great deal behind.

Beth, the daughter he'd barely gotten a chance to know. Paige had visited her in the hospital, where she'd stayed overnight to be treated for the flesh wound in her arm. She was going to be fine, Paige had said. A small scar that would make an interesting story to tell her children. His grandchildren.

He shook his head, his mouth twisting into a half smile beneath the dark mustache. Grandchildren. He still didn't quite believe he had a child. He wasn't ready for the possibility of grandchildren. Not that he'd know anything about it, he thought, the half smile fading.

When he left town this time, there was going to be no looking back. He'd made his peace with the past, though not in the way he'd hoped. He couldn't go back and change anything he'd done. He couldn't change what he'd been. He could only go forward from where he was now.

He'd even, in an odd way, made his peace with his parents. At nearly forty, he'd finally gotten it through his head that there was nothing he could do to change the way things had been. And nothing could change the way they were now.

He couldn't make his mother understand him or love him, any more than he could understand or love her. He'd spent twenty years trying and it hadn't worked. It had been foolish to think that it could all be changed in three months.

He'd done what he'd set out to do. Now all that was left was to say his goodbyes. And there were few enough of those to say. Pop was gone, the pain of his loss still raw. Martin had been a friend but he wouldn't be surprised to find Jake gone.

Beth. Yes, he wanted to say goodbye to Beth. He didn't think it was his imagination that she'd come to look on him as a friend. He owed her a chance to say farewell. Besides, he wanted to see her again.

That left only Paige. Paige. How was he supposed to say goodbye to her?

HE WAS NO CLOSER to an answer thirty minutes later as he rang the bell of the big white house. Frank answered the door, his eyes widening when he saw Jake.

"Hello, Frank. I'd like to see Beth."

"Jake." Frank stepped back to allow Jake to enter. But he didn't move to lead him upstairs, where he assumed Beth's room would be. "I didn't get a chance to thank you for what you did."

"If I hadn't been there, someone else would have been."

"But you were there and I want you to know I appreciate what you did. Beth... Well, she means the world to me."

He shoved his hands into the pockets of his trousers and Jake had the feeling it was to hide the fact that they weren't quite steady.

"Are you going to tell her?"

"No." Jake shook his head. "I don't think she'd welcome hearing that I'm her father. I'm leaving tomorrow morning and I just thought I'd say goodbye."

Frank's relief was almost palpable. "She's asked about you since the shooting."

"Frank? Who is it?" Josie's voice preceded her into the entryway. She came to a dead stop when she saw to whom her husband was talking. "What are you doing here?"

"He came to see Beth, Josie."

"Well, you can't see her." She moved forward, stopping next to Frank, her eyes dark with hatred.

"Josie." Frank's voice was stern.

"Well, he can't," she said petulantly, shrugging off his implied reprimand. "I don't want him anywhere near my daughter."

"Don't you mean *our* daughter, Josie?"

She paled at Jake's words.

"You can't tell her that! It would just about kill her to find out that Frank isn't her father. That her real father was a . . . a . . . murderer."

"Josie, that's enough!"

But it had been a long time since anything Josie said had had the power to hurt him. Jake smiled coldly.

"I was just telling Frank that I'd decided not to tell Beth the truth." He waited to see the flicker of relief in her eyes. "But I could still change my mind."

"Why don't you wait for me in the library, Josie," Frank suggested. "I'm going to take Jake up to see

Beth. No." He stifled her protest. "Not another word about it."

Josie looked as if she were going to say something more but perhaps it had finally occurred to her that she would do more harm than good if she did speak. With a final venomous leer at Jake, she went into the library.

Frank looked as if he felt he should say something but realized there really wasn't anything to say. He could hardly defend Josie. Neither could he criticize her.

"Beth's room is upstairs." He turned and Jake followed.

"How is she?" Jake followed him up the wide staircase.

"Remarkable." The paternal pride was so natural that Jake doubted Frank was even aware of it. "Her arm is healing just fine. And emotionally she's doing better every day. She's had a bit of trouble sleeping, though."

"That's not surprising," Jake said as they stopped outside Beth's door.

Frank looked at him, obviously struggling with something he wanted to say. "I want to thank you for not telling her, Jake. I should have told her years ago but it never seemed like the right time and then it seemed too late, somehow."

"You did what you thought was best."

"Yes. But I wouldn't blame you if you hated me."

"I don't hate you." Jake was surprised to realize that he didn't feel any bitterness about what he'd lost. Maybe it was a case of you can't lose what you've never had. "You probably did the best thing for her. I couldn't have given her the home, the stability that you have. She's a good kid, Frank. You did a good job."

Frank stared at Jake's outstretched hand for a moment before reaching out to take it.

"Thank you, Jake," he said, his voice slightly choked. "You're always welcome to visit, as a friend of the family."

"I don't think so. There's not much reason for me to come back here. And I don't think Josie would agree with you." His half smile took any criticism from the words.

"You're always welcome, Jake," Frank repeated. "I can handle Josie."

Jake waited until Frank had disappeared down the stairs before tapping on Beth's door. When she called to come in, he pushed open the door, stepping into a pretty, feminine bedroom in blue and white.

Beth was sitting up in the middle of the bed, her hair caught back with a headband, her face freshly scrubbed. When she saw him, her face lit in a smile and Jake felt a surprising ache. Her eyes were bright blue and it occurred to him that she'd gotten her eyes from him.

"Jake! Come in. Why haven't you come before?"

"I thought I ought to give you a little time to recover." He took the hand she held out to him, letting her pull him down onto the side of the bed.

"I *am* recovered. It's just that no one will believe me." Her faint pout changed into a more serious expression. "Dad told me that it was you who did the shooting last week."

"I wasn't the only one," Jake said.

"I should feel sorry that they're dead, I suppose." She'd kept hold of his fingers and her thumb worried absently at the back of his hand. "They were awful, Jake," she said, her voice a near whisper. "They laughed when they killed Pop. Such a sweet old man and they *enjoyed* killing him."

She lifted her head and Jake thought his heart would break at the tears that brimmed in her eyes. Acting on instinct, he put his hand behind her head and drew it to his shoulder, offering her the comfort of his strength.

"Try not to think about it, Beth. If Pop could have chosen a way to go, it would have been while he was trying to help someone. He wouldn't want you to dwell on his death."

"I suppose." She snuggled closer and Jake felt a sweet pain in his chest. She smelled faintly of powder. She must have smelled just as fresh when she was a baby. "Anyway, I want to thank you for what you did."

"I just happened to be there."

"If you hadn't been there, Lisa Mae or I would probably be dead right now."

"Well, you're not, so don't think about it."

She sat back and he had to fight the urge to pull her into his arms again, hold her just a moment longer to make up for all the years he hadn't been able to hold her. Her eyes were very direct as she looked at him.

"I know you don't want me to make a big deal out of this, Jake, but you did save my life. And I don't want you to feel bad about having to kill that man. They would never have let us go. You did what you had to do."

"Thanks for the pep talk," Jake said, his voice scratchy. He reached out to smooth back a stray lock of her hair. "But I didn't come by so you could reassure me. I wanted to see how you were and I wanted to say goodbye.''

He hadn't expected the word to hurt so much and it came out sounding forced. Beth's eyes widened.

''You're leaving?''

''Summer's over. It's time I move on.''

''Where are you going?''

''I don't know. I thought I might drive around the country a bit more, maybe head farther south where the weather will be a bit warmer.''

''Does Aunt Paige know?''

She was shrewd.

''I haven't told her yet,'' he said casually.

''I thought the two of you had something going.''

''I never planned to stay more than the summer,'' he said, sidestepping her comment.

''Don't you love her?''

She'd asked him that once before and he was no more prepared to answer that question now than he had been then. Love Paige? He didn't have any right to love her.

''You're nosy and you still don't have any manners,'' he told her lightly. He stood up. ''I'd better let you get some rest.''

''Any more rest and I'm going to go comatose,'' she groused. She caught his hand. ''I'm going to miss you.''

He looked down at her, feeling emotion catch in his throat. He'd known her such a short time. Just a few weeks out of her life.

''I'll . . .'' He had to stop and clear his throat. ''I'll miss you. For a tactless brat, you're not bad.''

''Gee, thanks.'' She grinned at him and then grew serious again. ''Will you write?''

Jake looked down at her, seeing himself in her eyes, in the shape of her chin.

Would he write? Hear about her life from a distance? The boyfriends he'd never meet, the graduations he wouldn't be there to applaud, the wedding where he wouldn't be the one to walk her down the aisle, the grandchildren he'd never hold.

He swallowed, forcing a smile.

"Sure, I'll write," he lied.

Standing outside her door a few minutes later, he thought he'd rather lose both arms than have to say such a difficult goodbye again.

And he still hadn't told Paige he was leaving.

HE KEPT TELLING HIMSELF that he was waiting for the right moment to tell her but that moment didn't seem to come. It certainly wasn't the right time to tell her over the dinner he'd prepared.

And after dinner wasn't the right time either. She took his hand to draw him into the living room. She turned the radio on, finding a station that played slow, dreamy music. Jake hadn't danced in more years than he could remember, but swaying in front of the fireplace with Paige in his arms, he felt as graceful as Fred Astaire.

She fit against him so perfectly, her head just under his chin, her slender body a sweet pressure on his chest, on his thighs.

His arms tightened convulsively around her. How could he possibly leave her?

Did he love her, Beth had asked.

Only if loving someone meant that the sun only came out when you were with that person. That you were only truly whole in their presence. If that's what it meant, then he loved her. Loved her so much it was like tearing away a part of himself to think about leaving her.

She'd said she loved him. If he asked her, would she go with him?

Yes. He didn't doubt it. But he wouldn't ask. He didn't know where he was going or what he was going to do with his life. She'd find someone who could give her all the things he couldn't. Someone young, with a few illusions left in him.

She'd be better off without him. But tonight... Tonight, she was his, only his.

His hand slipped into the silken length of her hair, tilting her head back for his kiss. She responded just as he'd known she would, melting against him, her arms coming up to circle his neck and draw him closer.

He wasn't going to think about tomorrow or the goodbyes he couldn't bring himself to say. Tonight they had all the time in the world. The future stretched out before them, rich and full.

There was a particular intensity to their lovemaking. Jake was saying with his body the words he couldn't bring himself to speak. He loved her. She was his soul, his only hope of happiness. Throughout the night he used his hands and mouth to tell her all these things.

It was nearly morning when Paige collapsed against his chest, her breathing ragged, her tears dampening his skin. Jake held her trembling body close, knowing he wouldn't sleep. He wanted to savor every moment he could. The warmth of her skin, the delicate scent of her hair. The memories were going to have to last him the rest of his life.

PAIGE FELT THE WAY his arms cradled her, holding her as if he would never let her go, and she knew he was leaving. Her tears fell silently, without fanfare. There'd been something different about him all night, a part of him she couldn't quite reach.

Somewhere in the intensity of their lovemaking, there'd been a note of finality. As if this was the last time they'd ever be together like this. He was trying to tell her goodbye. He hadn't been able to find the words but he didn't have to. She knew him so well. He'd become a part of her life, a part of her soul.

How was she supposed to go on without him?

IT WAS BROAD DAYLIGHT when Jake awoke, startled to find that he'd slept at all. His hand swept out searchingly. But the bed was empty. As empty as he felt.

A glance at the clock told him Paige should have opened the library nearly twenty minutes ago. She must have slipped out of bed and gone off to work.

He hadn't told her that he was leaving. He leaned back against the pillow, his forearm over his forehead. Perhaps it was just as well. He wasn't sure what would be worse: if she asked him to stay or if she didn't.

He could leave her a note, a coward's way out but perhaps easiest for both of them. God knows, he couldn't bring himself to face her again.

Jake dragged himself out of bed, his gaze lingering on the pillow that bore the imprint of Paige's head. He forced himself to turn away.

He dressed automatically, pulling on black jeans and a T-shirt before stomping his feet into the black leather boots he'd hardly worn since arriving at the beginning of the summer. Shrugging into his jacket, he took a last look around the old house.

The maple table he'd refinished sat proudly in the kitchen, restored to its former glory. He ran his fingers over the smooth finish. Would Paige think of him when she looked at it? Shaking his head, he hitched the duffel bag higher on his shoulder. More than likely, she'd take a hatchet to it, wishing it was his head.

He strode out the back door without looking back. The sun was warm but it lacked the strength of summer. Autumn had arrived. It was time he was moving on, time to decide what to do with the rest of his life. He had to give Paige a chance to get on with her life.

It was best this way.

He swung around the garage and came to a dead stop.

The Harley was parked just where he'd left it, facing into the street, ready for his departure. But leaning against it . . .

His gaze started at a pair of black leather boots and moved up an endless length of leg encased in skin-tight black denim. A snug black leather jacket fitted her waist, failing to hide the feminine curves. Her hair was braided and draped over one shoulder, white-blond against the black leather. Tucked under one arm was a black helmet with a tinted visor. There was even a pair of black leather gloves tucked into her jeans pocket.

"Where are we going?" She asked the question coolly, as if there were nothing else to discuss.

"*We're* not going anywhere," he said slowly, trying to regain his balance.

"Then why are we dressed like this?" She widened her eyes in surprise and Jake felt his mouth twitch.

"I was going to leave you a note."

"Well, now you won't have to," she said cheerfully. "I'm going with you."

"No, you're not."

"Don't you want me to go with you?"

"I—" He broke off, unable to utter the lie.

He scowled.

She was not impressed.

He tried harsh fact.

"I'm not good for you. I can't ever be what you need."

She was not visibly moved.

"Why don't you let me be the judge of what I need and what I don't need. I love you, Jake. I told you that before and I don't think you believed me. I guess I'm just going to have to tag along to convince you."

"Look, you don't really know who I am. You've got some romantic idea about me having traveled the globe, getting into romantic fights and killing people to save the world. That's not the way it was. I was little more than an assassin, a hired gun, a loaded cannon. I was a wind-up soldier for them to point at a target."

She didn't seem impressed. Jake ground his teeth.

"If they'd told me to shoot the President, I'd have done it without question."

"I don't believe you. And even if I did believe you, I don't think it's particularly important now. Are you planning on killing people as a hobby now that you've given it up as a profession?"

"No."

"Then we don't have a problem. I'm not interested in what you *were*, Jake. I'm only interested in what you are."

"And what do you think I am?"

"I think you're a man who's been hurt a lot. I think you've done things you regret. But I think you spend too much time thinking about them, instead of thinking of the good things in your life. You have a deep capacity for love, even if you won't admit it. You're stubborn and lonely and you take yourself too seriously. You're also kind and you have no tolerance for cruelty. And I love you."

Jake had never wanted anything in his life as much as he wanted to take her with him. He ached with the need to snatch her up and carry her off, to make her a part of his life forever. But he had no right to do that. He was still convinced she'd be better off without him.

Steeling himself, he forced the coldness into his voice.

"I don't want you. I'm sorry to have to be so blunt but I don't want you."

She didn't seem disturbed.

He watched her warily as she crossed the short distance between them. She laid one slim hand on his chest and Jake could feel that gentle pressure burning through his clothing until it seemed as if she were touching his heart.

"If you can look me right in the eye and tell me you don't love me, I'll let you go, Jake Quincannon. But you have to look me right in the eye and say it."

He stared into her eyes, bracing himself to say the words that would tear his world apart. His throat seemed to close. Her eyes were endless green pools, full of love and understanding and a faintly perceptible fear.

It was that tiny glimpse of fear that was his undoing. She'd bared herself to him, made herself completely vulnerable. He couldn't utter the lie that would crush that vulnerability. He'd told more lies in his life than he cared to remember, but this was one he couldn't tell.

He wanted her too much, needed her too desperately.

"Damn you," he said thickly.

He crushed her smile under his mouth, his arms holding her so tightly she could hardly breathe.

HALF OF RIVERBEND saw them leave town. Ethel Levine just happened to be in the window of Maisie's as the Harley roared up Maine Avenue. She described it afterward to half a dozen of her closest friends.

There was Jake Quincannon on that wicked-looking motorbike, wearing black leather and with that eye patch that made him look just like a pirate.

And perched behind him, looking happy as a cat with cream, was sweet little Paige Cudahy, her arms wrapped around his waist as if she didn't ever plan to let go.

Ethel shook her blue-haired head, her lips pursed.

Who would ever have thought that a good sensible girl like that would have her head turned by the likes of Jake Quincannon?

PASSPORT TO ROMANCE VACATION SWEEPSTAKES

OFFICIAL RULES

SWEEPSTAKES RULES AND REGULATIONS. NO PURCHASE NECESSARY.

HOW TO ENTER:

1. To enter, complete this official entry form and return with your invoice in the envelope provided, or print your name, address, telephone number and age on a plain piece of paper and mail to: Passport to Romance, P.O. Box #1397, Buffalo, N.Y. 14269-1397. No mechanically reproduced entries accepted.

2. All entries must be received by the Contest Closing Date, midnight, December 31, 1990 to be eligible.

3. Prizes: There will be ten (10) Grand Prizes awarded, each consisting of a choice of a trip for two people to: i) London, England (approximate retail value $5,050 U.S.); ii) England, Wales and Scotland (approximate retail value $6,400 U.S.); iii) Caribbean Cruise (approximate retail value $7,300 U.S.); iv) Hawaii (approximate retail value $ 9,550 U.S.); v) Greek Island Cruise in the Mediterranean (approximate retail value $12,250 U.S.); vi) France (approximate retail value $7,300 U.S.).

4. Any winner may choose to receive any trip or a cash alternative prize of $5,000.00 U.S. in lieu of the trip.

5. Odds of winning depend on number of entries received.

6. A random draw will be made by Nielsen Promotion Services, an independent judging organization on January 29, 1991, in Buffalo, N.Y., at 11:30 a.m. from all eligible entries received on or before the Contest Closing Date. Any Canadian entrants who are selected must correctly answer a time-limited, mathematical skill-testing question in order to win. Quebec residents may submit any litigation respecting the conduct and awarding of a prize in this contest to the Régie des loteries et courses du Quebec.

7. Full contest rules may be obtained by sending a stamped, self-addressed envelope to: "Passport to Romance Rules Request", P.O. Box 9998, Saint John, New Brunswick, E2L 4N4.

8. Payment of taxes other than air and hotel taxes is the sole responsibility of the winner.

9. Void where prohibited by law.

PASSPORT TO ROMANCE VACATION SWEEPSTAKES

OFFICIAL RULES

SWEEPSTAKES RULES AND REGULATIONS. NO PURCHASE NECESSARY.

HOW TO ENTER:

1. To enter, complete this official entry form and return with your invoice in the envelope provided, or print your name, address, telephone number and age on a plain piece of paper and mail to: Passport to Romance, P.O. Box #1397, Buffalo, N.Y. 14269-1397 No mechanically reproduced entries accepted.

2. All entries must be received by the Contest Closing Date, midnight, December 31, 1990 to be eligible.

3. Prizes: There will be ten (10) Grand Prizes awarded, each consisting of a choice of a trip for two people to: i) London, England (approximate retail value $5,050 U.S.); ii) England, Wales and Scotland (approximate retail value $6,400 U.S.); iii) Caribbean Cruise (approximate retail value $7,300 U.S.); iv) Hawaii (approximate retail value $ 9,550 U.S.); v) Greek Island Cruise in the Mediterranean (approximate retail value $12,250 U.S.); vi) France (approximate retail value $7,300 U.S.).

4. Any winner may choose to receive any trip or a cash alternative prize of $5,000.00 U.S. in lieu of the trip.

5. Odds of winning depend on number of entries received.

6. A random draw will be made by Nielsen Promotion Services, an independent judging organization on January 29, 1991, in Buffalo, N.Y., at 11:30 a.m. from all eligible entries received on or before the Contest Closing Date. Any Canadian entrants who are selected must correctly answer a time-limited, mathematical skill-testing question in order to win. Quebec residents may submit any litigation respecting the conduct and awarding of a prize in this contest to the Régie des loteries et courses du Quebec.

7. Full contest rules may be obtained by sending a stamped, self-addressed envelope to: "Passport to Romance Rules Request", P.O. Box 9998, Saint John, New Brunswick, E2L 4N4

8. Payment of taxes other than air and hotel taxes is the sole responsibility of the winner

9. Void where prohibited by law.

RLS-DIR

VACATION SWEEPSTAKES

Official Entry Form

MONTH 3 ENTRY

Yes, enter me in the drawing for one of ten Vacations-for-Two! If I'm a winner, I'll get my choice of any of the six different destinations being offered — and I won't have to decide until after I'm notified!

Return entries with invoice in envelope provided along with Daily Travel Allowance Voucher. Each book in your shipment has two entry forms — and the more you enter, the better your chance of winning!

Name _____

Address _____ Apt. _____

City _____ State/Prov. _____ Zip/Postal Code _____

Daytime phone number _____
                          Area Code

☐ I am enclosing a Daily Travel Allowance Voucher in the amount of $ _____ Write in amount revealed beneath scratch-off

© 1990 HARLEQUIN ENTERPRISES LTD.

VACATION SWEEPSTAKES

Official Entry Form

MONTH 3 ENTRY

Yes, enter me in the drawing for one of ten Vacations-for-Two! If I'm a winner, I'll get my choice of any of the six different destinations being offered — and I won't have to decide until after I'm notified!

Return entries with invoice in envelope provided along with Daily Travel Allowance Voucher. Each book in your shipment has two entry forms — and the more you enter, the better your chance of winning!

Name _____

Address _____ Apt. _____

City _____ State/Prov. _____ Zip/Postal Code _____

Daytime phone number _____
                          Area Code

☐ I am enclosing a Daily Travel Allowance Voucher in the amount of $ _____ Write in amount revealed beneath scratch-off

CPS-THREE